THE CHRISTMAS BEAR

B.N. RUNDELL

WOLFPACK
PUBLISHING
— EST 2013 —

The Christmas Bear

B.N. Rundell

Paperback Edition
Copyright © 2018 by B.N. Rundell

Wolfpack Publishing
6032 Wheat Penny Avenue
Las Vegas, NV 89122

wolfpackpublishing.com

Paperback ISBN 978-1-64119-602-4

Library of Congress Control Number: 2018964145

THE CHRISTMAS BEAR

THE GERMAN MGo8 MACHINE GUN WAS MERCILESS IN its continuous rat-a-tat-tat onslaught against the advancing 77th division of the First Army Corps. The men of the American division were staggering from bomb crater to tree stumps searching for any cover from the bloodletting. The screams of the wounded were punctuated by the blasts from the German trench mortars that exploded without pattern or mercy. Corporal Tom Turner lay on his back against the bank of a large crater, looking at the men coming from the trenches behind him. They reminded him of chickens in the barnyard, running in all directions, flapping their wings and squawking at anything and everything.

The shouted orders from Lieutenant Danvers caught his attention and he turned to look at the muddy bloodied face of his commander. Turner put his hand behind his ear and shouted, "What?"

"We've got to get that machine gun! Take two men and go to that crater at the foot of the hill! I'll take the others to this side an' we'll get 'em in a crossfire! Try to get a grenade into their hole!"

Turner nodded his understanding, motioned to the two men beside him, and lifted his head over the bank. The machine gun was raking the flats to his right and Turner brought his knees under him and jumped from the crater to start his run. He had taken no more than two long strides and a blast behind him knocked him to his face. He rolled toward another crater and saw the remains of the Lieutenant and the other men scattered in the crater he just left. They had taken a direct hit from the trench mortar of the Germans.

He lay on his belly, peering over the edge of the crater at the machine gun nest, watching it belch belt after belt of death dealing bullets into the ranks of the charging Americans. He surveyed the terrain between him and the gun and calculated his route to a possible cover site where he could assault the gun. Another look at the gun, wait till it swings away, and he was on his feet running to the next crater. He stumbled down into the muddy bottom and fell on his left shoulder, instinctively keeping his Springfield 30-06 rifle from the mud, but the slime splashed against his face and found the opening at his collar. He wiped the mud from his face, looked around and saw two dead and bloating Germans in the hole. He pushed away from the stench, looked over the lip of the crater to the machine gun, and plotted his next move.

He had to make it fast, that gun was killing men like it was mowing the grass in front of some rich man's palace and showing no more concern than a paid gardener trimming the hedges. Turner charged from his crater to a sizable stump and plopped down behind the upright protection. He noted this was the first stop that wasn't a mudhole and briefly considered staying right there until it was all over. But he sucked in a couple of deep breaths, took a quick look at the gun, and launched himself at the slope of the hill that was just out of sight of the men manning the MGo8. When he hit the hillside, he dug his toes in as he fought his way up the steep slope, fell forward and caught himself with the butt of his rifle, paused and took a couple more deep breaths, feeling his heart beating so rapidly he thought it would jump out of his chest. He waited a brief moment, gathered his thoughts and asked himself just what he was doing here anyway.

He changed his direction, thinking to come out behind the machine gun and have a better advantage. Cresting the hill, he was startled when a German soldier charged him with an outraged look on his face and a bayonet on his rifle. Turner quickly countered the rifle thrust with his own weapon and slashed down on the German's arm with his bayonet. The attacker screamed and started to bring his rifle butt up to strike him, but Turner countered, and the two men stood toe to toe, using their bayonets and rifles like cutlasses of two pirates, each screaming and yelling at the other.

Tom suddenly sat up, looking around in the dark room, and knew he was not on the battlefield, but in his own bedroom. He swung his feet over the edge of the bed, dropped his head into his hands, and breathed deep to calm himself. He looked over his shoulder as his wife, Amy, stirred and rolled to her side away from him. Tom stood to his feet, looked again at the still form of his wife, and tiptoed from the bedroom.

He moved by the light of the full moon streaming through the windows, stuffed his stockinged feet into his boots, slipped on his overcoat and stepped from the cabin into the cool of the night. He guessed it to be about two in the morning, too early to start feeding or milking the cow, so he strolled around the place. He stopped at the pole corral, leaned on the top rail, lifted his foot to the bottom rail and looked at the two bay mules and the lone dapple-grey gelding horse, all three standing hipshot, heads hanging and oblivious to anything around them. Images of the Meuse-Argonne battle intruded on his quiet moment and he remembered the sleepless nights spent in trenches and craters listening to the cries of the wounded and the sobs of the scared. He had read that his 77th division of the 1st Army had been successful in their campaign, but how the official count of 117,000 of the 1st Army were killed, or wounded could be counted successful, he didn't know. He was just glad, mighty glad, it was over. But he wasn't sure it would ever be over for him. The doctors called it battle fatigue, the troops called it shell-shock, but he called it nightmares. They seemed to come every night, reliving the horrific assault and seeing again and again the mutilated bodies he had to step over to continue the assault.

He lifted his head to the moon and slowly closed his eyes, soaking in the quiet of the night and the silvery glow that blanketed the countryside. He turned away from the corral and walked towards the cabin but moved to the side and walked to the back toward the tree line and two graves. One of the first things he did when he came home was to build a log bench that sat at the foot of the two graves and he dropped down on the bench and looked at the graves. The headstones read, "Wilbur Turner, 1851-1918, Winnifred 'Winnie' Turner, 1860-1917". These were the graves of his Mom and Dad. They had homesteaded this place, proved up on it, and had made it a good home, the only home Tom ever knew. But it had been a lot of work, clearing fields, building the cabin, adding on to the cabin, planting crops, building the barn and corrals, all the things that Tom now looked at in the moonlight.

When he had been conscripted into the army, Tom was fearful that his hardworking father would not be able to take care of the place by himself and might work himself to death. It wasn't the work, but a broken heart, that did him in after losing his beloved wife of forty years to pneumonia. Tom's wife, Amy, and their children, Tammy, and Tom Jr. stayed with his folks when he went to war. Tom and Amy had proved up on the adjoining 160 acres and Tom was building a new home but was conscripted before he got very far and now this was their home, but they were faced with a lot of challenges. Not the least of which was that Tom's father had taken out a loan for some livestock from the Chaffee County Bank and it was overdue and Tom didn't know if they could make the payment. If they couldn't, they stood to lose everything. He dropped his head into his hands and began to pray.

"Good morning, Daddy," proclaimed the blonde topped seven-year-old standing in the barn door in her green calico dress. She was holding the egg basket at her side, having gathered the chickens' offerings for the day.

"Bout time you got up, sleepyhead!" chastised her nine-year-old brother, Tommy. He was balanced on the three-legged stool, head leaning against the side of the guernsey cross milk cow as he squeezed and pulled on the teats to fill up the milk bucket. His corduroy britches were held up with suspenders over his green plaid felt shirt.

"Good morning, Tammy," answered Tom as he forked some hay to the horse and mules.

"Mom's got breakfast ready!" declared Tammy as she turned to go back to the cabin, blonde curls bouncing.

"You 'bout got that done?" asked Tom as he looked to his son, Tom Jr., "We need to get breakfast done so you won't be late for school."

"Ah, the only thing good 'bout school is it's almost time for Christmas vacation. Mrs. Parks is beginnin' to look like a Christmas tree, her hair was green yesterday! All she needed was a string o' popcorn and an angel on her head and we could stand her in the corner an' put presents under her!"

"That's no way to talk about your teacher! She puts up with a lot from you and your hoodlum friends. It's no wonder her hair turns different colors!"

"It don't turn colors, Pa, she dyes it. Kids are startin' to take bets on what color it's gonna

be from day to day!" he muttered as he started to stand and lift the milk pail from under the cow. He pushed her tail from under his bent knee, kept there to keep her from slapping him across the face with a wet manure laden tail as milk cows are known to do. He stepped back, almost stepping on a barn cat's tail, stumbled and caught his balance, spilling only a little of the milk before catching himself on the stall sides, but not before his foot landed in a fresh cow pie. "Aaach, great! Now I'm gonna be smellin' all day!"

Tom chuckled at his son's dilemma and said, "All ya gotta do is use the brush and some water, it'll wash off easy 'nuff." He stepped to his son's side and took the milk pail, dropping his other hand on the boy's shoulder. "If that's the worst thing that happens to you today, you'll be alright." They walked together to the house, stopping at the wash basin sitting on the shelf on the side of the cabin nearest the well to wash up for breakfast.

As Tom pumped the water, he looked at the mountains and the snow that sat above timberline. The foothills that marked the end of their property held a few patches of snow on the shaded slopes, but so far this winter, they only had a couple of snows that left any accumulation. The fields beyond the barn were bare of snow, but the stubs of the corn showed, and the gleanings were feeding the thirty head of cattle. Across the fence the other field showed grass and alfalfa stubs, but little enough for the animals. He was hoping for more snow in the mountains and on his fields to give a better yield for all his crops in the coming summer, if they were still here, he thought.

The cold water splashed on his face took his breath away, but he stood up and grabbed for the towel before the cool morning breeze made it worse. Little Tommy had the towel in hand and kept it out of reach of his dad who had his eyes closed as he searched, but Tommy's laughter told him of the often-pulled trick and a swooping arch of his arm caught the young perpetrator and snatched the towel from the hands of the giggling culprit. Once his face was dry, Tom saw his son bend over for the milk pail and he quickly snapped the towel on his behind with a pop that made the boy straighten up with a "Yow!"

As the two men of the house stepped through the door, both chuckling, Amy turned to see them laughing and looking at the table. "It's about time you two got in here, it's getting cold already!" she declared as she grabbed the cast iron skillet and started slipping the fried eggs onto their plates. When everyone was seated, they joined hands and Tom nodded to little Tommy and the boy began, "Thank you God for our food and our Momma that cooked it. Thank you for this day and be with me'n Tammy as we go to school. Amen."

Amy shook her head in wonder as she passed the platter with the sausage and bacon. Tom forked off his share and passed the plate to little Tommy as he accepted the basket of biscuits from his wife. It was a sumptuous breakfast and the usual fare for the family. Small talk circled the table and Tammy asked, "Are you gonna take us to school, Daddy?"

"Yes, sweetheart, we'll be taking the wagon into town and we'll drop you and your brother at school. Mom and I have to go on to Salida, but we'll be back by the time school's out and pick you up. So, today, you get a ride both ways!"

"Goody! It's starting to get too cold to walk to school anyway," she mumbled around the last bite of the biscuit with apple butter.

"Don't talk with your mouth full, sweetie," gently scolded her mother.

"Whatcha gotta go to Salida for, Dad?" asked Tommy.

"Oh, gotta see a feller 'bout some business, that's all."

"Oh, I get it, Christmas is coming ain't it?"

"Isn't it," corrected Amy.

"That's what I said," answered Tommy, looking at his Mom.

"No, you said 'ain't' and you should say 'isn't' instead."

"Oh," answered the boy, scowling at the remains of his biscuit. He reached for the apple butter and smeared the last bite, popping it into his mouth as he started to get up.

"Have you been excused?" asked his mother.

"Uh, oh, may I be excused?" he responded.

"Yes, you may, and get your book and slate because we're leaving right away."

THE MULES LEANED INTO THEIR HALF-SWEENEY collars, pulling the traces taut and rattling the trace chains, as they pulled the buckboard from the barn. Tom pulled the wagon alongside the cabin and hopped down to help his family into the wagon. He hoisted Tommy and Tammy into the back, "You two bundle up with that quilt, now, it's getting cold out." He turned, and his big form overshadowed his wife, her petite figure swallowed up in the bear hug of her six-foot tall broad-shouldered husband. He rested his chin atop her head and held her tight and she put her arms around his sides, unable to completely reach around him, and lay her face against his chest. "Alright you two, we gotta get to school!" reprimanded little Tommy, laughing at his parents. Tom lifted Amy up to the buckboard seat, waited till she was situated, and walked around, stepped on the hub of the front wheel and climbed into his seat. Amy flipped the end of the quilt over his lap as he picked up the reins and slapped the mules' rumps to get started.

It was a little less than two miles to the school house that stood across from their church and other children were already waiting at the door. Tammy and Tommy jumped down, carrying their slates, books and lunch pails, and with a quick "bye" and a wave, they joined the group at the door. A slap of the reins and Tom and Amy started down the road into Poncha and on toward Salida.

"Do you really think the bank will let us make the smaller payment?" asked a worried Amy, leaning closer to her man. She pulled the quilt tight against her thigh to keep the breeze from chilling her.

"I really don't know, hon, all we can do is try."

"You'd think Mr. Randall, being a deacon at the church an' all, would be a little more understanding. It's not your fault your father borrowed the money, and it's not your fault we had such a dry summer. If we'd had more rain, your corn and hay would have been better and..."

"I know, I know, but that's the way business works. Especially banks nowadays, they're only interested in making more money and not helping their neighbors. Even this bank, why, when I was still home, Mr. Randall was as helpful as could be, but now..."

"It's like he's mad at everybody because they lost their son in the war. It must be a terrible thing to lose a child like that, of course you'd know more about that than I would, but for him to take it out on the rest of the community, it's just not right, and like the pastor says, it's just not Christian," declared Amy with a half-hearted attempt at stomping her foot on the toe board. "And you've been working so hard at the lumber mill and the livery an' all, you can't do any more. How much can we give him this time?"

"Well, last night we counted out $128, and I figger if we give him an even hundred, until after the first of the year, he should be willing to settle for that."

"But how much are we supposed to pay?"

"Well, the agreement Pa had with the bank was to pay $150 a year for five years. That paid for the cattle and the balance of the other note he had from before. If he'll settle for this payment this time, we should be alright. The cows are all bred, and we should have a good calf crop and if we get good snowfall and a wet spring, we should do well with the other crops. But if he's still cantankerous, I don't know..."

THE BUSINESS DISTRICT OF SALIDA WAS SHOWING considerable growth, especially since the end of the war. Chaffee County Bank, the large stone two story building, sat on the corner of 4th and Main and was the most imposing building in the small district. Tom pulled the wagon to the side on 4th street and tied the mules off to the hitchrail beside the boardwalk. The street showed ruts from other wagons in the week before but now a dust devil danced at the far corner telling of the dry nature of winter. Tom lifted Amy down from the wagon and set her tiny feet in her lace up shoes on the boardwalk. "I'm going to B & F Drygoods for some material and you know how those ladies like to talk. I'm sure I'll still be there when you're done, but if not, you'll find me next door at the Dress shop. And don't worry, I'll not be buying anything at the dress shop, I just want to visit with Dorothy for a bit. She told me last Sunday that she might want Eleanor to take some piano lessons, so we'll see."

Tom turned from the hitchrail and with one foot up on the boardwalk answered, "Well, I'm hopin' this won't take long, but the way J.B.'s been lately, he'll probably make me 'cool my heels' for a bit 'fore he talks to me."

"Well, you just mind your manners, and don't lose your temper, 'cause that won't do us any good, for sure." She tiptoed up to give him a peck on the cheek and he bent to meet her. He watched her walk away and around the corner before he stepped up on the boardwalk and readied himself for his meeting with the banker.

He mounted the wide grey granite steps that led to the big double doors set at the corner of the building. Gold Leaf letters on the door windows boldly proclaimed, *Chaffee County Bank, J.B. Randall, President.* Tom pushed open the big oaken door and stepped into the warm interior. Along the left side were three barred teller cages that ended with a waist-high bannister railing that cordoned off the back of the main room. As he looked at the barred cages he remembered what his father said about all bankers should be behind bars. He chuckled as he looked around. Another door with *J.B. Randall* written in an ark on the frosted window, told of another office beyond. Tom walked to the railing and was greeted by a rather small man with a green eyeshade over piercing black eyes. His shirtsleeves were bloused with garters and his vest framed his string tie that dangled at an awkward angle from his shirt that was missing a button and below his starched collar. The clerk looked up at Tom and asked in a rather feminine voice, "Yes?"

Tom stood with his hat in his hand before him, cleared his throat, and said, "I'd like to see J.B."

"If you mean Mr. Randall, do you have an appointment?"

"No, I don't have an appointment, but I'd still like to see him. It's about a note we have with the bank."

"Well," flustered the mousy clerk, "if you just need to make a payment, I can take care of that!"

"No, I need to speak to J.B.." stated Tom, rather firmly.

With a shrug, the clerk rose, cast a rather superior look at Tom and turned to the office door. He rapped twice, bent his ear close to the glass, and opened the door. He closed it behind him and Tom could hear muffled voices beyond. Within moments, the door opened, and the skinny clerk walked to Tom and said, "It will be a while before Mr. Randall can see you, if you want to wait," and motioning toward the row of chairs along the wall, "you can be seated there."

Tom looked at the clerk and the door beyond, then turned to the chairs. He took off his plaid Mackinaw and laid it on the chair beside him, set his hat on top and sat back with arms folded across his chest and glared at the clerk who dropped his eyes to the papers on his desk.

It was at least a quarter hour later before a bellow from the office rattled the windows and the clerk jumped in his chair. "Send that man in!" came the order from the president of the bank. The sheepish clerk motioned to Tom and walked to the railing to swing the gate open for Tom to enter. The clerk motioned to the door and Tom strode confidently to the door, turned the knob and pushed it open.

Sitting behind a massive and paper-strewn desk was a rather portly man with thinning grey hair, clean shaven face with a ruddy complexion, and sporting a worsted blue suit with a vest. A gold watch chain and jeweled fob decorated the front of the vest, and a bow tie peeked from under a tall starched collar. Thick eyebrows drew down as he scowled at the younger man that stood before him, "Alright, what is it?" he growled.

"Well, J.B., I came to make a payment on that note of my

father's," said Tom as he reached into his pants pocket for the bills. He counted out the one hundred dollars on the corner of the desk as the skeptical eyes watched and J.B. leaned back in the chair that squeaked in protest. Tom was startled when J.B. hollered for his clerk to, "Bring in that Turner file!"

When the meek clerk stepped through the door and carefully slid the file onto the corner of the big desk, Tom stepped back and dropped his hands to his side. The big man cleared his throat, reached for the file and flipped through the pages, then lifted his eyes to Tom, "According to this note, you're to pay $150! You've only got $100 there!"

"That's right, J.B.," started Tom but was interrupted by the portly president, "It's Mr. Randall to you!"

Tom shifted his weight from one foot to the other and crossed his arms across his chest, took a deep breath and said, "I know the note calls for $150, and it's not due until the end of the month. But with the poor summer and all, I was hopin' you'd give us more time."

"Time? The terms of the note are set and if you can't make the payments as agreed, then I'll have to start foreclosure proceedings!" growled J.B.

"Foreclosure? Over $50? You can't be serious?!" responded Tom, leaning on the edge of the desk and raising his voice slightly. He was shocked that the man who had been known as a friend to his family, an upright member and deacon of their church, would take such a drastic measure in such circumstances.

"The terms of the note are quite clear! And I'm tired of so many of you people thinking you can just do as you please! I'm trying to run a bank here, not a charity!"

"But I'm working two jobs trying to make the money. What else can I do?"

"That's your problem, not mine," he looked away from Tom and hollered for his clerk. When the man came back into the office, the president said, "Make out a receipt to Turner here for $100 payable on their loan and make a note that the loan is in default!"

"It's not in default!" declared Tom just as forcibly as did the president, "It's not in default until the end of the month and then only if the payment is not made!"

J.B. sputtered and shuffled papers and looked at his clerk, "According to these papers, this note has been in default ever since your father missed a payment, uh, let me see, yes, he only made a partial payment at the end of last year! So, it is in default!"

"That can't be! My father always kept his bills paid!"

"Not according to this!" he declared, pounding on the papers before him. "So, for your note to be current, you must pay $125 by the end of this month. And if you fail, I will start foreclosure!"

Tom stood aghast and speechless before the man. This was a complete surprise and he could think of nothing to say but dropped his head and looked at his hands as he stood, unmoving.

The clerk quickly scribbled the receipt, tore it from the pad and started to extend it to Tom but had it snatched from his hand by J.B., who looked it over, and with a "Harumph! Here! Now, I'm busy!" and waved his hand to dismiss both the clerk and Tom.

Tom went to the chair, picked up his hat and slipped on his Mackinaw, turning toward the door, shaking his head all the time. The three tellers watched as Tom turned, dropped their heads and shuffled papers as Tom exited the bank. He was relieved there were no other customers in the bank to hear the confrontation with the president, but he was dejected after the warning from J.B. His mind was racing, searching for ideas or some way out of this dilemma, some way to meet the note payment. As was his habit, he spoke quietly to his Lord. *What am I going to do, God? What little money we have we need to live on, and between now and Christmas, I won't make enough to make up the difference. We can't lose the home place, Lord, we don't have anywhere else to go!*

As his foot hit the last of the grey granite steps, he almost ran into his wife coming around the corner from the dry goods store. "Oh, well, maybe you should be watching where you're going! You almost knocked me down!" chided Amy as she looked at her man.

"Oh, I'm sorry sweetheart! I was just thinking and not looking." He reached his arm around her waist and pulled her closer. "Have I told you how beautiful you are?"

She could tell he was trying to turn her attention away from him, but she played along, "No, I don't think I've heard you say that in a very long time!" She cocked her head to the side and acted a bit coy as she answered.

"Now, I've heard women have poor memories, but that takes the cake. I distinctly remember telling you how beautiful you were just this morning. And if I remember correctly, it's when you were passing the biscuits!"

"Oh, I thought you were talking about my biscuits!" she answered with a mischievous smile. This type of banter was common for them and she relished the times of kidding one another but using those times to tell of their love for one another. And she dearly loved this man, the father of their two beautiful children. They had been sweethearts since the third grade and she cherished every memory, including the times when he dunked her pigtails in the inkwell of their desks at school. Her thoughts went quickly to the times in the big brick school house and when they shared their lunches as they sat on the swings, side by side. Her father was the preacher at the church when they were younger but had recently retired and surrendered his pulpit to a young man fresh from seminary and full of ideas. Times had changed as they always do, and now with all the responsibilities of a family, it seemed their fun times were few and far between. They had learned to take each moment as a precious gift and cherish their times together. This was one of those moments.

They mounted the seat of the wagon, wrapped the quilt around their legs and started back home, quietly enjoying the closeness. As they left town, Tom's eyes naturally turned to the mountains and the clouds, hoping for snow, at least enough to begin to accumulate and provide enough watershed for the summer months. They desperately needed a good summer, but those thoughts brought him back to the immediate need of the note with the bank. *What can I do? I've got to think of something! I have to!*

Amy could tell Tom was disconcerted, but she chose to allow him the time he needed to sort out his thoughts. She knew he would tell her what was on his heart when he felt he was ready, but that he needed her support in the meantime. With the short days of winter, the sun had settled just behind the mountains when they pulled up to the big brick schoolhouse. Tammy and Tommy sat with the teacher, Mrs. Parks, on the top step, waiting. They jumped up and waved at the first sight of the wagon and scrambled up the sides as soon as the wagon stopped moving.

"Thanks for waiting with them, Mrs. Parks," said Amy, "I hope it wasn't long."

"Oh no, it's just been a short while, and we had a nice talk, all about Christmas and the Christmas play that we'll be doing this year at the church. Both of the children will be a part of it this year, won't they?" asked the matronly woman as she stood straight and tall in her straight-line skirt. She hugged her fur-collared coat close and glanced at the disappearing sun as it painted the sky above the mountains.

"I'm sure they will. And thank you again!" answered Amy as the wagon started moving. She saw the teacher wave as she stepped down from the porch and started toward her house that was nearby. Amy thought about the Christmas program, knowing she had a lot of work to do since she was the piano player and had to know all the music. She looked over at Tom, saw he had slipped into his deep thinking and quickly worded a prayer for her family and the challenges they would face in the coming days.

"But Pa, I thought we was gonna go fishin' today!" declared a frustrated Tommy sitting across the breakfast table from his Dad.

"Sorry, buddy, but I've got to work today," answered an equally frustrated Tom.

"Ahh, that's all you ever do, is work," muttered the boy, feigning a pout with a wrinkled forehead and a pooch mouth. Then a sudden idea struck, "What about after work?" he asked with a hopeful expression painting his face.

"Nope, then I gotta go to the Livery and help ol' Thaddeus. I'm sorry buddy, maybe after Christmas things'll be better and we can go fishin' and huntin', how 'bout that?"

"Oh, alright, I guess. I reckon I got plenty o' chores to do anyhow," he grumbled as he forked the last bite of egg into his already crowded mouth. He wiped his plate with the last piece of biscuit, mopping up all the egg yoke and held it in readiness as he finished off his current mouth full.

"Besides, you'll be lookin' after your sister for a while. I'm meeting Dorothy and Eleanor at the school for Eleanor's first piano lesson, but it won't be for long." Said his Mother as she looked directly at Tommy and leaned toward him and shook her finger, "I'm counting on you, young man."

"That's fine, Ma, I'll put her to work muckin' out the stalls. That'll take her a good hour and a half at least!"

"Ma, Pa! He can't make me do that! Eeewww, those stalls are full of manure and they stink!" complained Tammy as she scowled at her brother.

"Don't worry, Tammy, he won't make you muck the stalls. He knows that's no job for a lady," declared his mother, laughing at the pair. She picked up the empty plates and started for the sink and as soon as her back was turned, Tammy stuck her tongue out at her brother, who laughed and picked up his plate and cup to carry to the sink.

"I'll hitch up the team and be back in just a bit," said Tom as he stepped behind his wife and put his arms around her waist and pulled her close.

"Well, you better let me go so I can be ready, I've still got things to do!" she answered with a giggle and turned to give her husband a peck on the lips. She looked to Tammy, "And you, young lady, you will do the dishes while your brother mucks out the stalls, understand?"

"Yes, Momma, anything as long as it's not those smelly ol' stalls!" she answered as she wrinkled her nose for emphasis.

"And, when you're done with that, you can do the dusting, and no reading until you're done!" said Amy with a tilt of her head to her daughter.

"Alright, I will," answered a slightly contrite Tammy, scooting from her chair and starting to the sink. One of the first improvements that Tom tackled when he came home from the war was to put a pump inside the house which was somewhat of a luxury for the times. Tammy stood on the stool that put her at the right height for the sink and stretched for the pump handle and started the up and down to get the water flowing. When she had about four inches of water in the sink, her Mom came to her side with the teapot full of hot water and warmed up the dishwater with about half of what was in the pot.

"Thank you, Momma," said Tammy as she reached for the dishrag and started her work.

The door pushed open and the cool December air filled the cabin as Tom asked, "You ready, woman?"

"Woman, is it?! You better change your tone if you want this fair lady to ride in your wagon mister!" declared a grinning Amy as she stood with one hand on her hip and the other holding her purse and papers.

"Yes m'am! Then, how 'bout the fair lady of the house bein' such a beautiful woman care to ride in my wagon this morning?" asked Tom as he bowed at the waist and swished his hat to the floor and back again, smiling broadly at his bride.

"Well, I suppose, since you're such the gallant gentleman!"

Amy kissed Tammy on her cheek and started for the door, went to the wagon and called out, "Tommy, Tommy! We're leaving!"

The boy stepped to the door of the barn, pitchfork in hand and hollered back, "See ya!"

DOROTHY AND ELEANOR WERE WAITING INSIDE THE clapboard church building and greeted Amy when she stepped through the door. A fire was going in the stove and the room was nice and warm as Amy hung her coat at the back and walked to the front where the others waited. As she looked, she noticed the church had been decorated in a

Christmas theme with hand-made wreaths, snowflakes, and more. There was a small table top that held the manger and hand made figures for the wise men, Mary and Joseph, the Christ child and the animals. The piano sat to the right of the pulpit and her mind went back to the many times she played for the services and her father had preached the messages. But tomorrow would be the first time for the new pastor and she was uncertain how the people would accept the change. She looked at Eleanor, already seated on the piano bench, smiling in anticipation of her first lesson.

"Well, you look excited, are you anxious to begin?" asked Amy as she neared the piano. The red-headed freckle faced girl nodded her head enthusiastically and answered, "Yes ma'am."

"Well, good," started Amy as she sat on the bench with Eleanor and placed a book on the piano. "This is your first book, it's the classic First lessons for Beginners from C. Schirmer. We'll start right here in the beginning," she explained as she looked over her shoulder at Eleanor's mother, Dorothy, who smiled and nodded her head at her friend.

The lesson was over all too soon, and after asking her mother's permission, Eleanor ran outside to spend some time on the swings while the women visited. They had been best friends for several years and as Amy sat on the front row of seats beside her friend, Dorothy asked, "What's the matter, Amy, you look a little down. Is everything alright?"

Amy dropped her eyes and shook her head, "Oh, I don't know. I've just got a lot on my mind, what with Christmas coming and all."

Dorothy looked at her friend and waited for more but as she watched Amy dab at her eyes with a small handkerchief she knew there was more, "Come on, you can tell me. I'm your best friend, remember? And what are friends for if not to share burdens? Now, what is it?"

Amy's shoulder's shook as she took a deep breath and looked at her friend, "Oh, I probably shouldn't say it, but, well, we went to the bank yesterday and got a bit of a shock. Apparently, Tom's dad wasn't current on the note like we thought, and now, we might lose the place because of it."

"Oh no, Amy, no. Oh, surely Mr. Randall could work something out for you, won't he?"

"That's just it, ever since he lost his son in the war, he's a different person. Tom said he was belligerent and refused to give any leeway. If we don't make the payment by the end of this month, he's going to foreclose!"

"Oh, Amy, I had no idea."

"We didn't either. Tom went to make a payment and ask for some time, but when Mr. Randall said there was more due because of the back payment of his dad, Tom just didn't know what to say, and the banker told him to leave!"

"Oh my," declared Dorothy, scooting closer to her friend and putting her arm around her shoulder to pull her close.

Amy dropped her head to Dorothy's shoulder and let a sob escape, lifted up and wiped her eyes as she looked at her friend, "Please, don't say anything to anyone about this, please?"

"Of course not, you know me better than that. I won't tell a soul, but, I will be praying for you. Do you think there's any way you'll be able to make the payment?"

"I don't know, I hope so, Tom's working two jobs and we're trying to think of anything else that we can do, but we'll just have to wait and see. Thanks Dorothy, it helps just to talk about it."

. . .

As she walked along the road towards home, Amy fingered the dollar bill in her pocket, glad that she could do something to help, little though it was, *All I need is a hundred more students between now and Christmas and it'll amount to something,* she thought. She looked around at the few cottonwoods that lined the roadway and stretched their skeletal limbs to the cloudy sky. Between the road and the mountains, the valley cradled the South Arkansas River, or as the locals knew it, Little River, that split the meadows down the middle. She could see the buildings of their small farm or ranch as Tom called it, and the ponderosa and spruce that served as a windbreak around and behind the house. It was a homey setting and she had quickly grown to love it, although she and Tom had only known it as theirs for about six months, just since he mustered out of the army and came home. She had done her best to keep things up after Tom's dad died in February until Tom came home in May, but it was after the family was together that it had really become their home.

She saw the two children playing something in front of the house as she neared and soon recognized it as hopscotch. Tammy was hopping on one foot as Tommy watched, neither had seen their mother, and Tommy jumped up, pointing to the squares, "You stepped on the line! You gotta go back!"

"I did not!"

"Uh huh! Look! There's your footprint, there, on the line, see?" declared Tommy, pointing to the foul.

Their Mom laughed at the two, who upon hearing her approach turned to look, and said, "That's enough! Now, we need to have some lunch and start getting things ready for your baths and for church tomorrow."

Tommy's chores were to feed and water the horse,

mules and milk cow and bring in some wood for the stove. Tammy helped her mother maneuver the bathtub into the kitchen area and started filling it with water, while her mother stoked up the stove and heated some water. By the time Tom got home, the children had finished their baths and their supper and had been tucked into bed. It was a tired and dirty Tom that came through the door, but he smiled widely as he was greeted by his wife, who announced "Everything is done! The animals are fed and watered, the wood's in, and your bath is ready, oh great master!" as she curtsied with bowed head as if she were a servant. She giggled as she looked up at her dirty faced husband and added, "And you sure need it!"

Tom grabbed her anyway and rubbed his face against hers and kissed her full on the lips. She squirmed but gladly kissed him back and as they pulled apart, she waved her hand in front of her face and said, "That's enough! You get in that tub and clean up. It'll probably take you all night just to scrub yourself clean!"

"You mean I've got to take a bath before I eat?" he asked, flabbergasted.

"How 'bout you scrub, and I'll give you something to eat while you scrub?"

He grinned and started stripping off his shirt and readying himself for the tub. Amy added some hot water just before he stepped in and set the pot back on the stove before she went to the counter to fetch him a slice of meat and a biscuit. He made short work of both the biscuit and the bath and they were soon sitting side by side in front of the fireplace, holding hands.

Amy handed her husband the dollar bill and said, "Well, that's one less dollar we have to worry about."

"You mean she paid you a dollar just for a piano lesson?" he asked.

"That's right! My talent and my time is worth something, don't you know?"

He hugged her close to him and said, "Ever little bit helps, sweetheart. Now all we gotta do is figger out how we're gonna get the rest of it."

"Do you really think we can do it, Tom?" asked Amy, leaning her head on his shoulder.

"We have to babe, we can't lose this place. It's our home. I've been thinkin' 'bout it all day and I don't have the answer, but we'll just keep at it. I'm sure the note is just on the home place and not against the other 160, but, we don't have a house there and besides, we just can't lose this, it's our home now. We'll work it out somehow, it might take everything we can do, but somehow..."

Tommy sat up in bed, his place in the loft was always warmer than below, but he also heard everything anyone said when they were below him. He frowned as he thought about the possibility of their losing their home. *Surely not,* he thought, *we can't lose our home.* And he began thinking about what his dad had said about doing everything they can to keep it. He was trying to think of something he could do to help when he lay back and fell asleep.

Tom and Amy held hands and bowed their heads and Tom began to pray, *Dear Lord, we have a lot to be thankful for and we are very grateful for all your blessings. But now, we come to you with a heavy burden and it's one that only you can handle.* He emptied his heart before his Lord and as husband and wife committed their burden to the Lord, they held each other close, knowing that all of their tomorrows were in the Lord's hands.

THE COMMUNITY CHURCH OF PONCHA SPRINGS WAS not unlike many other small-town churches of the time. The white clapboard church building and it's bell-tower with the cross on top stood as a landmark and most everyone in the community attended every Sunday. This Sunday was extra special as it was the first Sunday for their new Pastor, Reverend Allen Davis and his wife, Rebekah. Pastor Davis had recently graduated from Southern Seminary in Louisville, Kentucky, and the west was still considered a mission field. When Pastor Edwards decided to retire, he contacted his alma mater, Southern Seminary, and asked for a replacement. Pastor Davis had always been fascinated with the west and enthusiastically accepted the assignment.

"Alright, you two, go get in the wagon. Your Mom an' I will be out in a minute, and don't get dirty! You know your Mom'll tan your hides if you do!" declared Tom, grinning as he motioned to the youngsters.

"Ah, Pa, Ma ain't never tanned our hides, she just makes you do it, you know that!" chided Tommy as he ran through the door, watching over his shoulder for any retaliation from his father.

Tom just chuckled as he turned to Amy, "See there, your kids know the truth of it! They know who's boss in this house!"

"Do you want me to throw this Bible at you?" asked Amy as she picked it up from the table. Her draw-string purse dangled from her wrist as she reached for the Bible and the sheets of music. She didn't know exactly what the new Pastor would want for the music portion of the service, but she wanted to be prepared. Tom held the door for his wife and as she stepped near he bent to steal a kiss saying, "You sure look pretty today, little lady!"

"Why thank you, kind sir. And may I say you're looking pretty handsome as well?"

"You may!" he answered as he lifted her up to the seat on the wagon.

BEHIND THE SCHOOL/CHURCH BUILDING WAS A LONG three-sided shed with corrals for the horses and ample room beside to park the wagons and buggies. Sunday was usually a full day, with a pot-luck dinner that followed the service and sometimes an additional time of singing and fellowship, with kids playing games and adults sharing news afterwards. Today would be a get acquainted time for the new pastor and his wife and everyone was looking forward to the day.

When Tom pulled the wagon near the front steps, he reined up and got down to help Amy and the kids to the ground before he took the wagon around back and put the horses up in the corral. Parked to the side of the shed were three vehicles, a big green touring car with a radiator emblem that said Stephens was a new addition and Tom was certain this belonged to J.B. Randall, the banker who enjoyed showing off his wealth. The other two were both Model T's, with the touring model belonging to the McPherson's, the owners of the grocery store, and the runabout belonging to Mr. Armbruster, the owner of the Jackson Hotel. Tom shook his head at the thought that Henry Ford said the Model T was made for the masses, but in these times just after the war, few of the "masses" could afford the $500 for an automobile.

Several of their neighbors were arriving and the greetings flowed, and a sweet spirit of expectancy filled the air. After he greeted several of their friends that were already seated, Tom took the seat at the end of the row next to Tommy and Tammy and nodded at his wife, seated at the piano.

Most everyone made it a point to walk around and greet each other before they took a seat and it was expected of the leaders of the church to set the example, but Tom noted that J.B. Randall, the chairman of the deacon board, was seated with his wife and had not taken part in the time of greeting one another. As Tom thought about J. B. and his recent meeting with him, he also remembered that since shortly after Tom returned from the war, J.B. had become rather acrimonious in his manner with everyone. Tom knew that J.B.'s son, John Jr., had been one of the 117,000 that died in the battle of the Argonne, he had been in the same 77th division as Tom, but Tom didn't know that until after he came home. He also thought J.B. had been rather surly to every one of the returning soldiers, almost as if he blamed them for the death of his son, or that he resented their coming home when all he had of his son, was a marker at his grave.

To begin the service, another one of the deacons, Mr. Armbruster, the owner of the Jackson Hotel, walked to the pulpit and raised his hands to quiet the crowd. Tom saw several of the other deacons with their families, the McPherson's that owned the grocery store, and the Burnett's, whose father had been the first Indian agent and had homesteaded the ranch where the family now lived. Tom also nodded a greeting to the Hutchinson's, one of the oldest families in the area and Mr. Hutchinson also served as a deacon. There was another church in town, but this was the most popular and drew most of the prominent people. Even J.B., who was the president and founder of the bank, had a ranch about half way between Salida and Poncha, up on the mesa, and he had always attended this church. Tom grinned as Donovan Armbruster, now with everyone watching, motioned for the people to stand and nodded to the pianist, Amy, to begin the first song, *Shall We Gather at the River*.

As the song ended, Armbruster had everyone be seated and began, "I am pleased to see everyone today on this very special day for our church and our community. As you know, this is the first Sunday for our new pastor," and he nodded toward the pastor, seated in a high-backed chair behind him and to his right, "the Reverend Allen Davis. Pastor Davis is a graduate of the Southern Seminary of Louisville, Kentucky, and has long had a desire to come to the west. We are happy to welcome Pastor Davis and his lovely wife, Rebekah, to our community and our church." He nodded toward Rebekah, looked at the people and started clapping and everyone joined in the applause.

"Now, before our pastor comes, let's have one more song, a rather new one that has a very special message, *The Old*

Rugged Cross." He motioned for everyone to stand and nodded to Amy to begin.

THE PASTOR STEPPED TO THE PULPIT WEARING A GREY worsted suit with a matching vest and began with, "Thank you everyone for that fine welcome, and although today seems to be about me and my wife, it really isn't, for every time we come together our attention should always be on the Lord Jesus Christ. So, let us turn in our Bibles to Matthew chapter 22 and begin with verse 35." Everyone stood and the shuffling of pages turning was heard as they searched for the proper passage and when their collective eyes lifted, the pastor began reading. When he finished with verse 40, he motioned for everyone to be seated and began his message with a brief introduction of the setting of the time and said, "But let us focus our attention on the last part of verse 39, *Thou shalt love thy neighbor as thyself."*

His message was simple and straightforward, expounding on the emphasis placed on the command by Jesus when he said, *On these two commandments hang all the law and the prophets.* Then he added, "When we love others as ourselves, we will be just as concerned for their welfare as our own. For example, when you got dressed this morning to come to church on this cool December morning, didn't you put on warm clothes? But did you even think about your neighbor and wonder if they had warm clothes to wear? And what about food on the table, if you have food on your table, shouldn't your neighbor also have food? So, you see, beloved, Jesus really meant it when he said we were to love our neighbor. And by the way, love is an action not a feeling, it's what we do, not what we feel. So, as we near the Christmas season, should we be concerned about what's under our Christmas tree, or should we be concerned about our neighbor?"

Tom smiled as he saw J.B. squirming in his seat but knew he couldn't pass the message by himself. He was concerned about his family and the situation with the bank note, but he also realized he should be just as concerned about his neighbor and lately he had been too busy to even visit with his neighbors, much less to see how they were doing. The pastor had said when you love another, you put them first and he had to ask himself if he had really done that and his answer didn't sit well.

THE AIR WAS COOL, AND THE CLOUDS HAD ROLLED IN and appeared to be threatening a snow storm as Tom and family climbed into the wagon to start for home. The day had been a wonderful get together with friends and to meet the new pastor, but everyone needed to get home before dark and with the days in December being so short, the festivities had been cut short. They were pulling away from the church when Amy leaned toward Tom, tucking the quilt around their legs, and said, "The pastor and Rebekah will be coming to dinner tomorrow, can you come home in time?"

"Well, that was fast. How come we rate the first visit?"

"Rebekah wants to organize the Christmas program and she wanted time to talk with me about it. They'll be visiting folks quite a bit in the coming days and she just wants to have things organized. And the pastor wants to talk about the music also, and I think he might have something up his sleeve for you to do also."

Tom turned to look at his wife with a look of alarm, "What? What do you mean, something for me?"

"I'm not sure, but I'm thinkin' he's one that wants everyone involved, so, you might want to talk to the Lord about it before they get here."

"Oh, so now you're all gangin' up on me, is it?" he asked, pretending to be upset, but having a hard time holding back a smile. They both knew that Tom had a hard time saying no to anyone that asked for his help.

TOMMY AND CODY WALKED SIDE BY SIDE MAKING THEIR way home from school, followed by Tammy and Clarissa. Cody and Clarissa were twins and their parents, John and Millicent McPherson, owned the grocery store. The McPherson home was about half way between the school and the Turner home and the four children often walked to and from school together and since the twins and Tommy were the same age, Cody and Tommy had become best friends. Clarissa had taken Tammy as an adopted little sister and the four had become as close as if they were all brothers and sisters.

Nine-year-old fourth grade boys are too big to be little and too little to be big. Big enough and old enough to have responsibilities called chores, but small enough not to be trusted to exercise their independence without supervision. But that didn't stop the boys from getting caught up in the age-old game of one-upmanship and they had a round of it going as they walked home.

"No, you can't!" declared Cody. "A .22 isn't big enough to take deer huntin'!"

"Yes, you can, my Pa did! He took that .22 Marlin rifle out when he was huntin' and got him a deer with it!" argued Tommy.

"When did he do that?" asked his adversary, Cody.

"When he was younger, prob'ly my age. He said his Pa's 25-35 was too big for him, so he took the .22. Got him a buck, too!"

Cody looked sidelong at his friend, wondering about the veracity of his remark but decided to ask, "Did you ever shoot the .22?"

"Yup, Pa took me out a couple times an' we shot it. He said I was a good shot an' mebbe we'd go huntin' together sometime soon."

"Wow, my Pa says I gotta be 10 'fore he'll let me shoot. That's not till next summer," he stated a little downhearted, kicking at a rock in the road. He looked up and saw the road to their place and turned to his friend, "See ya' tomorrow!" and took his sister's hand as they turned down their roadway.

"Wait up, Tommy," came the frail voice of Tammy, quickening her pace to catch up with her brother. Tommy stopped and turned around to wait for his sister, only a few feet behind him but to a seven-year-old with short legs, it was a long distance, and she did not want to walk alone.

"Well, come on, slowpoke. We got chores to do!" encouraged the big brother. He smiled as his sister stretched out her hand to take his, so they could walk together the rest of the way home. Their mother sat on the top step watching as they came down the last few yards of their road and waved as she stood to welcome them home. She stooped to give each one a big hug and asked, "So, how was school today?"

Tammy immediately and excitedly said, "I won, Momma, I won!"

"You did? Great! What did you win?"

"I won the spelldown! Mrs. Parks had the first three grades go against each other, and I won!" she explained as she jumped up and down, making her blonde curls bounce on her shoulders.

Amy hugged the excited girl, "I'm so proud of you! That's wonderful!" She turned to Tommy and asked, "And how was your day?"

"Oh, alright. Nuttin' special, just school." The boy was not one to show too much excitement, but Amy knew he was a good student and enjoyed school, even though he tried not to show it, thinking he was too old for that. Amy ran her fingers through his wavy blonde hair and said, "Well, I'm proud of you too! Now, you too get out of your school clothes and get your chores done. We've got company coming for supper!"

Tommy lifted his eyes to his mother, "Who's comin'?"

"The pastor and his wife, and your Pa's supposed to be home early too. So, don't dilly-dally, I'll need your help."

Tom had been home just long enough to get out of his work clothes and get washed up before the pastor and his wife pulled up in front of their house in a single seat buggy with the top up and drawn by a high stepping black gelding. Tom stepped from the porch and took the horse by the reins, holding him steady while the pastor stepped down and helped his wife down.

"Welcome, Pastor and ma'am. You folks go right on in, I'll put your horse in the corral and let him get some water and hay, if that's alright?"

"Thank you, Tom. That would be fine."

Amy had stepped out on the porch and spoke up, "Welcome Pastor, Rebekah. You folks come right on in, we're pleased to have you visit. Supper's almost ready." She showed them into the house, directed them to the divan and asked, "Would you like some coffee or tea?"

"Oh no, we'll just wait till the meal. Thank you," answered Rebekah, "May I help with anything?"

AFTER THE MEAL, THE WOMEN BUSIED THEMSELVES with the clean-up and the men retired to the divan and the Pastor finally broached the subject of Tom's involvement in the church. "So, tell me, Tom, how long has your family been a part of Community Church?"

"Well, Pastor, like we said earlier, my family home-steaded this place goin' on thirty years back. I proved up on the adjoining 160 just 'fore I went to the war. But, my family's been a part of the church as long as we been here. Now the Presbyterian church was here 'fore our church, but I don't remember my folks ever goin' there. So, this here church is the only one I've known."

The pastor was several years younger than Tom, but his education had equipped him well for the ministry, but his life experiences were a little on the light side and he was well aware of his shortcomings, but his enthusiasm made up for his lack of experience. He smiled at Tom's explanation, and replied, "I find that fascinating. When I was younger, my family moved around a lot, my father was also in the ministry and his calling took him to different locations. So, I'm somewhat envious of you and the roots you have here. And you have a very comfortable home and a fine family as well.

"Your wife told Rebekah that you were rather skilled in woodworking, is that right?"

"Well, I do like to work with my hands. I get a lot of satisfaction out of creating things. I got that from my Pa I reckon," said Tom as he motioned around the room, "Most of the furnishings you see were made by either my Pa or me," explained Tom, finding it comfortable to talk about familiar things. He wasn't sure what to expect in a one-on-one with the pastor, as he was never comfortable trying to discuss biblical topics. He knew the Scriptures, and knew what he believed, but trying to explain it to others made him uncomfortable, as did any kind of talking before crowds. He was concerned the pastor was going to ask him to teach a Sunday School class or something that required speaking before others and he was not about to condescend to that. He looked to the pastor and waited, searching for words that could get him out of any kind of job that made him uncomfortable.

"Well, Tom, Rebekah and I have been talking about the Christmas program and I'm sure she's talking about it now with Amy. There's only a couple of weeks left, and we want it to be the best program possible. Now, here's what I would like to ask of you." He paused as he noticed Tom tense up a bit, but continued, "With your skill at woodworking, could you possibly help with the sets? You know, the backgrounds for the program, the manger and such."

Tom didn't realize he was holding his breath, but when the pastor explained, he was relieved it was something that he could do without speaking before others, and he let out his breath and let a slow smile spread across his face. "Well, Pastor, that is something that I could do, but I'm not sure about the time. You see, I'm working two jobs as well as taking care of this place and I usually leave the house before first light and don't get home till dark. But, if it's not too much, maybe I could find a few hours to work on it."

"You're working two jobs?" asked the Pastor, concerned.

"Yessir, you see, while I was gone, things were a little difficult and my father had to get a loan from the bank in town. I knew about it, but I thought it was current because my Pa had always been careful about those things. But when I met with J.B., he told me it wasn't current and the amount I owe is considerably more than we expected. So, I'm doing what I can to make extra."

"J.B.? Do you mean Mr. Randall?"

"Yessir, he's the president of the bank. If I don't make the payment, he said he would have to start foreclosure and we would lose our home. So, I have to do whatever I can to take care of that, and that leaves little extra time. But, I should be able to get the sets made up for you."

"Well, surely, Mr. Randall would give you some leeway, wouldn't he?"

"I'm sorry, Pastor, I really shouldn't have said as much as I did, but I wanted you to understand about my time."

Pastor Davis looked at Tom, considered for a moment, and said, "I see. I understand, and if you find that you can't, please let me know. I've done a little carpentry myself and maybe I can help." He turned to his wife and said, "Rebekah? Are you ladies about done with all your planning on the program?"

She turned to her husband as she dried her hands with a dishtowel, "Yes dear, I think we've got it pretty well thought out. Amy here is a Godsend, with her talent and knowing everyone, I think we have all the parts filled and she will even help with the costumes. So, yes, I'm ready if you are."

Tommy and Tammy had been sent to bed shortly after supper, as they usually were, but Tommy, in his loft bed over the living area, had listened to the conversation between the pastor and his father. He rolled to his side and started thinking. *We can't lose our home! Pa always said, we have to do everything we can, so, what can I do to help? There's got to be something.* And with thoughts of helping his family to keep their home, he slowly drifted off to sleep.

"ALRIGHT CHILDREN, NOW MRS. DAVIS, THE NEW pastor's wife, has asked that all the children that are a part of the Community Church, to go to the church as soon as you're dismissed. The ladies are preparing the Christmas program and they want you to be a part. Isn't that wonderful?" Mrs. Parks clapped her hands and looked at each of the children in her class. The school had two teachers and Mrs. Parks taught first through sixth grades, and Mrs. Burnett taught seventh through twelfth. Although the big two-story school building had been built in 1883, and the town of Poncha Springs was growing at the time, two tragic and massive fires had all but wiped out the entire town. Now there were fewer students and two teachers were able to teach all twelve grades that had only twenty-eight students, sixteen in the lower grades and twelve in the upper grades.

"Bundle up now, it's getting pretty chilly out there. Tommy, button up that coat, and Samuel, you too." She looked over her charges, satisfied they were all properly done up and said, "Alright, Cody, you may open the door. Bye now, children, I'll see you tomorrow!"

As the front door opened, the wind whistled through and every child grabbed at their coats, ducked their heads and pushed their way through the doorway. Most of the children, twelve in all, walked straight across the street and clambered up the stairs and into the church doors. Dorothy Leggitt served as the door monitor and hustled the children inside and quickly shut the door.

"Welcome, boys and girls!" declared Rebekah, with Amy standing at her side. "Now, everyone, take a seat here in these first two rows, and we'll get started." She motioned to the two rows on the right side of the church, the same side as the piano, and watched as the children scrambled for seats, each wanting to be by their best friends. As they settled down, Rebekah stood before them and began, "Now, we ladies have the program planned, and we, or maybe I should say Mrs. Leggitt and Mrs. Turner, have determined which one of you should be in each part. Now, when we tell you the part we want you to try, please take your places as the ladies direct you, understand?" She watched as heads nodded, some more enthusiastically than others. As in any group, there were those that were excited about being in the program, and others that were either fearful or disinterested, but all had been instructed by their parents to cooperate.

As Rebekah rattled off the names and the roles, the children took their places. There were four shepherds, three wisemen, one angel, the innkeeper and his wife, and Mary and Joseph. Cody and Clarissa were to be Joseph and Mary, Tommy and Eleanor were chosen as the innkeeper and his wife, Tammy the angel, and the other children doubled as the wisemen, shepherds and choir. Two girls had to serve as shepherds and one, Susanna Holman, whined, "But we can't be shepherds, we're girls!"

"You certainly are! And, there were times that the shepherds had their wives join them, so it's quite alright for you to have the roles as their wives. Besides, we need some good voices among the shepherds to sing one of the most important songs in the program! Would you do that for us, please?" asked Rebekah, with a broad smile as she looked at the girls. Susanna smiled and nodded her head as she stepped back to take her place among the shepherds.

The first practice was mostly to get the children familiar with their places and roles, finding their position on the platform, and a run-through of the songs and the lines. The practice went well, and all the children seemed to be happy with their roles as they chattered excitedly while they were gathering their things and putting on their coats. The ladies followed suit and as they exited the church, everyone ducked their chins into their collars and scattered in the different directions to make their way home.

Tommy and Cody led the way, with Clarissa and Tammy, holding hands with her Mom, following. The cold air was a challenge and cheeks and noses were showing pink when Cody and Clarissa waved goodbye and started down their roadway. Tommy, Tammy, and their Mom drew closer together, the children flanking their Mom and mittened hands holding tight. As they passed the corner of the fence, Amy stopped and shaded her eyes, looking in the distance to the far corner of the larger field. The children looked up at their Mom, then turned to look where she was staring.

"Those are turkey buzzards, ain't they?" asked Tommy, also shielding his eyes from the glare of the rapidly setting sun.

"Yes, they are, and it looks like something is down out

there. I hope it's not one of the cows, that's the last thing we need." She dropped her hand and took up the mittened paw of Tammy, "Come on children, we need to get in the house before we freeze!" The trio started walking faster as they neared the porch of the house. Quickly mounting the stairs, Amy pushed the door open and ushered her children inside, swiftly shutting the door to stay the cold.

She went to the stove, opened the door and stirred up the coals, added some kindling and the flames soon jumped to life allowing her to put in some larger pieces of wood and closing the door, she backed up to the stove, hands behind her, to absorb the heat. The children mimicked their Mom, one on each side as they stomped their feet and soaked up the warmth. Amy was deep in thought when Tommy asked, "You think I should go check out what them buzzards were after? If'n it's one of the cows, it might just be down and not dead. If that's all it is, them buzzards need to be shooed off, don't they?"

Amy looked down at her big little man and nodded her head. "But you get out of your school clothes, first!" she admonished. As he started up the ladder to the loft, she added, "And don't take too long, the light's fading and I want you back in the house before dark."

"Yes ma'am," answered the boy as he disappeared into the loft.

HE REACHED UP TO TAKE THE MARLIN MODEL 18, .22 rifle from the pegs. He turned and saw his mother's concerned expression and he explained, "It's just to scare them buzzards away. And if there's a coyote or sumpin' else, this will help scare them too."

"Well, you just be careful. I know you know how to use that, but be careful anyway, understand?"

"Yes ma'am." He stood the rifle by the door, put his scarf around his neck and slipped his arms into his coat. His mom put his stocking cap on his head and pulled it down over his ears, helped him to button up and stood back. He reached for the .22, opened the door and walked out without a word. This was one of those responsibilities that fell to the boy with his father still at work. By the time his Pa made it home, it would be too dark to see what was happening in the far field, so Tommy had to do the job.

He set the rifle against the fence post and struggled with the loop of wire that secured the end post of the pasture gate. Once open, he stepped through, and used the wire secured lever stick to pull the gate taut and dropped the loop over the top of the post. He reached through and grabbed his rifle and started to the far end of the pasture. With the rifle cradled in his arm, he ducked his head to the wind and with an occasional peek from under the upturned collar, he found his way to the log bridge that spanned Little River. Although called a river because it was the south fork of the Arkansas, by size it didn't measure up to be a river, more of a big creek. Not over a foot to eighteen inches deep and spanning about fifteen to eighteen feet, the river held fast to the icy shelves along its banks, the only evidence of the season. He looked up to see three deer, a young buck and two does, scramble away from their evening drink from the river.

Once across the bridge, Tommy looked toward the object of the buzzards and dropped the rifle to his hand, readying to use it to scare off the carrion eaters. As he neared, a coyote turned and bared his teeth, head lowered, to warn off the intruder. Tommy lifted the rifle and squeezed off a shot that put the bullet between the front legs of the coyote, sending the cowardly beast on his way. The shot also made the buzzards fly and Tommy barely caught sight of a badger that turned and skittered away. The boy approached the carcass slowly, searching the area for any other predators.

The dead animal was one of the pregnant cows that was part of the herd of hopes of his family. The stench of death and rotting meat filled his nostrils and he tucked his nose back behind his collar, but walked slowly around the dead cow, surveying the carcass for cause of death. It was evident it had been attacked by either a cougar or a bear, the neck and rump showed an abundance of claw and teeth marks, and the belly had been ripped open. What he saw he knew was not from the buzzards and coyotes, but some bigger predator that was capable of taking down a full-sized cow.

Seeing nothing that he could do, Tommy looked skyward and saw several buzzards circling, biding their time. He scanned the nearby tree line for any other predators and saw nothing. The coyote had disappeared into the brush by the fence line. In frustration, Tommy lifted the rifle and took a random shot at the buzzards, more to vent his emotions than to take down a predator. His shot went wild and he dropped his eyes and started back to the house.

Tommy reported to his Mom and handed off the .22 to turn to his chores. He still had to feed the horses, mule, and milk cow, a task that was a part of his normal routine and one he took pride in, except on days that were cold, and darkness was pressing upon him, like today. It was dark in the barn and he lit the lantern before forking the hay to the horses, although their stalls were empty and would be till his Pa came home. He checked on Bossy, the milk cow, threw her a forkful, and went back to the lantern to blow out the light and get inside to a warm fire. He was wondering just what his dad would say about the cow when he looked up to see his Pa pulling into the yard with the wagon and horses.

"Hi Pa!"

"Hello Tommy!"

"I've already put the hay out for the horses, so they'll be fine. I'm goin' inside to the stove!"

"Alright, tell your Ma I'll be right in soon's I put the horses up."

"Kay, Pa," answered the boy, quickening his step to get free of the cold chill. The warm stove beckoned him, and he was anxious to warm his hands and feet and get some warm food. He chuckled to himself, *Now I'm soundin' like Pa!*

"IF IT'S EVERYTHING THAT TOMMY SAYS IT IS, WE HAVE us a problem. We can't afford to lose even the one cow, but we sure 'nuff can't lose any more!" declared Tom as he sat across from his wife. The table was covered with an oilcloth and he absent mindedly traced the outline of the floral design as he pondered the situation. He looked up at Amy, "I'm just gonna have to take a day off and take care o'things. That carcass needs to be buried or at least drug off into the timber. And whatever it was that killed it needs to be hunted down 'fore he gets another'n."

Amy stretched her hand across the table and looked at her husband with sympathetic eyes, "Doesn't seem like we have much choice, does it? Like you said, those things hafta be done, and I sure can't do it and Tommy can't either."

"Yeah, I know. But I was also thinkin' 'bout that note at the bank. What with losin' this cow, we can't afford to butcher another'n, and without that meat, what're we gonna do?"

"Well, maybe you'll see a deer while you're out after whatever killed the cow? There's nothing wrong with us eating venison, matter of fact, I kinda like it," she answered with a smile.

"Since when?"

"Well, while you were gone, your Ma taught me a thing or two about cookin' venison and she made it taste pretty good, what with gravy an' such," she explained with a firm nod of her head to emphasize her point.

"Well, maybe so, but you can't cook it unless I get it. What with that cougar or bear prowlin' around, the deer are liable to be pretty skittish." He looked up at his wife again and shaking his head, "It musta been a cougar, I mean, all the bears are s'posed to be hibernatin' ain't they?"

"Aren't they," she corrected, "but yes I believe the bears should be hibernating. However, our winter so far has been pretty open and fair, so there might be a lone bear that's still looking to fatten up before he turns in for the winter."

"Yeah, you're right. But I'll check over that carcass and see if I can't tell if it was a cougar or bear, and maybe there'll be some tracks around to tell me. But for now, I think we need to turn in 'cause tomorrow's gonna be kinda busy." He stood and took her hand to lead her to their bedroom. Upstairs in the loft, Tommy rolled over and thought about what his folks had said about the bank note, needing meat, and about deer or venison. Maybe tomorrow his Pa would let him go with him and the two of them could bag a deer for their meat as well as get the varmint that killed the cow. Maybe.

AMY STEPPED OUT ON THE PORCH, HOLDING HER WRAP about her shoulders as she watched her husband returning from town. He drove the wagon to the barn, waving at her as he passed. She knew he had given the kids a ride into school and he was to go to the mill and ask for the day off to tend to matters in the field. Apparently, he had been successful and would be preparing to go on his quest. She turned back into the house to ready him some food to take with him for the day. She had already spent time in prayer for him and the duties for the day, now she would have to do what she could to help her man. She glanced at the rifle on the rack above the fireplace as she walked to the kitchen counter, and in that moment, she uttered another quick prayer for his safety.

She was almost finished with the sandwiches when she felt the breeze come through the open door and she knew Tom had come in from the barn. He stepped behind her and put his arms around her waist, "And how is my lovely today?"

"Oh, a little anxious, I guess. Just concerned about you and that animal out there. You will be careful, won't you?"

"Of course. You know me, I'm not one to take chances with anything, but you know it's gotta be done," explained Tom as he stepped away and started gathering his gear for the day. "I've saddled up Meg, she's a little more surefooted than either of the horses and she's not as skittish either," explained Tom, knowing his wife would be concerned all day until he returned. Anything he could do to assure her of his safety, he would do just to give her a little less to worry about.

She saw him reach for the rifle and asked, "Is that thing big enough to take a bear?" She had heard talk about the different rifles and had heard Tom express his wish to buy a bigger caliber rifle for hunting, but they had never had the extra money to indulge his wants. Now she was concerned for his safety.

"Well, it's not a big gun as far as guns go, but if I'm careful and place my shots well, it'll kill anything I hit."

"Even a bear, especially one of those Grizzlies?"

Tom chuckled, "Babe, there's not many Grizzlies around these parts anymore. Not that there couldn't be, but it's been a long time since anybody's talked about seein' one. So, I'm not worried about that, but if there is a stray one hangin' around and he ain't hibernating like he should be, then yes, this little .25-35 could kill it. Might take a little doin' but it could."

"Oh, that's definitely reassuring. Promise me if you see a Grizzly you'll hightail it home!"

"Now, that's not what I'm goin' out for, just to see somethin' and run back home!"

"You know what I mean!" she declared with hands on her hips and her head tilted.

"Yes, I do. But don't go worryin' your little head 'bout something that ain't gonna happen, O.K.?" he added as he packed his saddlebags with the food. He added a bedroll to his gear, just in case he had to spend the night, and with rifle and scabbard in one hand, the bedroll and bags in the other, he stepped through the door, held open by his wife. The mule was tethered in front of the porch and he tied all the gear down and turned back to his wife, shivering in the cold with a thin wrap about her shoulders. He pulled her close and gave her a kiss, leaned back and smiled, "Don't worry, I'll be back 'fore you know it. But if for whatever reason I have to spend the night, don't trouble yourself, I'll be fine. Understand?"

Not trusting herself to respond, she simply nodded her head and pushed him away. "Now be off with you. The sooner you leave, the sooner you'll be back!"

. . .

THE CARRION EATERS HAD BEEN BUSY. ALL THE INSIDES of the cow were gone, ribs were picked clean, the meat on the haunches and shoulders had been picked over, the eyes were picked out and little remained of the carcass. Some of the buzzards had hopped away and now stood looking on from about fifteen yards. He had seen a coyote scurry off as he approached but there were no others within sight. But he stepped down for a closer look and as he examined the hide just in front of the tail, he saw wide spread claw marks and puncture marks from the teeth of the predator that took the cow down. He could see where the cow had been taken from the rear, and the attacker had reached farther along the back for a second claw hold. This action was typical of a cougar that could take the animal on the run, grabbing first atop the haunches, then reaching farther forward for a better claw hold, until he could tear at the rear with his rear paws and cripple the cow for it to fall and then a choke hold on the throat to throttle the dying animal. He was certain, this cow had been killed by a cougar or mountain lion.

He lifted his eyes to calculate the time based on the position of the sun, then back at the carcass. Usually, a cougar would drag it's kill to cover, bury it with nearby debris, and return to the kill. But this cow was too big to drag, and the cougar might have returned in the night, but there was little left for a return feeding. He would have to go on the hunt, even though the cougar might still be close by, it was going to be difficult to try to track something that did little to leave sign of its passing. Suddenly, a crying yeowl split the silence and Tom recognized the cry of the cougar. It must be nearby and expressing his anger at others on his kill.

The mule, a little nervous already as it stood near the stench of death, lifted his head and began wobbling his ears back and forth, searching the trees beyond the fence-line for the source of the ruckus. The cougar let out another cry, followed by a couple of barks or spats, and Tom grabbed up the reins of the mule, "Come on Meg, I know where that critter is now!" He swung aboard and pulled the mule's head around to head to the corner gate to get out of the pasture and into the woods.

The cry of a cougar can carry a considerable distance, and a worried Amy, who was pacing the porch and praying for her man, lifted her head at the distant sound. She wasn't sure what she heard, and she stood frozen, waiting. When the cry came again, she shielded her eyes to see the small shadowy figure of her husband mounting the mule and take off at a run for the corner gate. *Oh Lord, please, keep him safe! He has to come back to me, please?!* She looked, trying to see more, but he was too far away. She could only assume he was on the trail of that cougar and he was in danger. A man is no match for the craftiest killer in the woods.

Tom secured the gate, mounted the mule and started for the tree line. He knew it was not the normal behavior of a mountain lion to make his presence known during the daylight hours and that cry would seldom be heard except during a night hunt. But this one was a mystery to Tom, as it was also unusual for a lion to go after a cow, especially one so near civilization. If the cow had been part of a herd that had been put out on a grazing lease in the forest or other government land, that seemed to make them fair game for the cougars and bears, but this one had been awful brazen to come into the pasture so near to houses and people. As he thought about it, Meg was picking her way up the mountainside trail, and he remembered some of the old-timers talking about how old tom cougars would turn to easier prey that they could take down without an extended hunt and stalk. Or cougars that had been injured, either in a fight with others or maybe wounded by hunters, would also go after domestic stock.

Meg stopped suddenly, lifting her head, ears forward and nostrils flaring. Tom leaned forward, searching the trees and rocks for any movement. He knew exactly where they were. Just beyond the edge of these aspen was a huge rock formation with little vegetation and lots of crevices and even some caves or overhangs that could be a cougar's lair.

He whispered to Meg, "Easy now girl, hold steady, I'm gettin' down." He grabbed the rifle from the scabbard, swung his leg over her rump and stepped down to the ground. He was watching the trees and the rocks beyond for any movement, but seeing none, he led Meg to a nearby tree and tethered her with a slip knot, just enough to keep her here, but loose enough that if she was attacked she could pull loose.

He stepped carefully, knowing that if the cougar was nearby he had already caught his scent, but he wasn't anxious to give the predator any more advantage than he already had by knowing exactly where the man moved. He stepped beside a big ponderosa, leaned against the trunk and surveyed the rocky formation ahead. He knew cougars were always on the hunt and never thought defensively. They would take the highest point where they could see all around them and from which they could launch an attack. Tom searched for that point and decided on two or three places on the rocky knoll that would fit that description. He searched it again and decided his choices were sound. Now he had to determine his route, some way to get to higher ground or at least keep from having to expose himself to an attack from above or from one of those promontories he had picked.

He looked back at Meg, fidgeting in the small clearing by the tree he had used as a tether, then back at the knoll. He decided on his route and slowly moved back into the thicker timber, then started off on a trot that would take him out on the top and backside of the knoll. He just hoped Meg would be safe for that long, but he was counting on the cougar picking up the scent of the mule and losing the scent of the man.

His route took him about a half-mile around the flank of the knoll and up through a cut in the rocks and out behind the top of the promontory. He stopped beside another tall ponderosa to catch his breath, he was breathing hard from the unusual exertion and had to ready himself. He searched the rocks before him and knew the wide flat-top would make for silent moving, as long as he didn't slip or drag his boots that would make a scraping sound and give him away. Once he was rested and breathing normally, he decided to drop to all fours, rifle slung on his back, and crawl forward, a move that brought back memories of the war. And just like then, any noise could be deadly, so he moved slowly and stealthily. As he neared the edge, he slowed and carefully peered over, searching for movement.

It was nothing but the twitch of the tail of the big cat, but it was enough for Tom to spot his quarry. The big cat had a perfect look-out and based on the position of his head, Tom was certain he was watching the mule back in the trees below. With the cat about twenty yards below, Tom carefully slipped his rifle from his back to ready a shot. As he brought the rifle around, he slowly jacked the lever to be certain there was a shell in the chamber but saw none and finished the movement to bring a cartridge into the chamber. He saw the shell move into the chamber and slowly and as quietly as possible, he pulled the lever back to seat the cartridge and ready his shot. But the click as he set the lever caught the cat's attention and it swiftly turned to look and launched itself off the ledge. Tom brought the rifle to his shoulder and in one smooth movement, he brought the sight to bear and squeezed off a shot at the fleeing cougar. He heard the bullet strike, saw the twitch and twist of the cat and knew he had scored a hit. But when the cat landed on the ground below, he took off into the timber, only slightly hindered by his wound.

Tom jumped to his feet, spotted a quicker route off the rocks, and jumped, slid, skidded, and leaped to get to the bottom and give chase. He looked to the woods in the direction the cat had taken, quickly searched the ground and found spots of blood. He looked at the trail, back at the mule and turned to get his mount to give chase.

Meg was showing her nervousness, but Tom could sense she was excited about the hunt as well. He was also certain that if he had left her tethered to the tree, she wouldn't be there when he got back. He leaned over the side to check the trail, still seeing a few spots of blood, they continued their pursuit. Several times he had to stop and go back to pick up the trail from the last place where they saw blood, but even though the progress was slow, it was progress. Tom was in no hurry to come upon a wounded and desperate cougar but was more than willing to bide their time and hopefully find a dead carcass that would present no danger.

When they came to a wide expanse of slide rock, Tom stepped down, looked to the sun and back to the slide rock then turned to Meg, "Let's take us a break for lunch, O.K. Meg? I ain't too excited about this slide area, too many spots for that cat to be hidin', and if I'm gonna get jumped, I'd just as soon it be on a full stomach. Don't you think?"

Meg looked at the man, flipped her ears back and forth, and waited for his action. Tom tethered the mule on a long lead, so she could crop some grass, loosened the girth, and grabbed the saddlebags with his lunch. All the while he munched on his lunch, he was hoping the lion would stop and bleed out so all he had to do was find it, skin it, and take it home. But he was skeptical of his chances for such an easy outcome.

Once he finished his lunch break, he tightened the girth and took the long lead, tucked the end in his belt at his back and started across the slide rock. His caution was simply to prevent the mule having to cross with the burden of man on his back, and assured Tom that the mule wouldn't spook or slip and cause the both of them to go down. With the many sizeable rocks in the slide, there were also many places the lion could be holed up and waiting and he wanted to be ready with rifle in hand. He carefully placed his feet for each step on the wobbly moss-covered slide rocks, searching the area ahead for movement. The rifle had a round in the chamber, but the hammer was lowered with his thumb ready to bring it to full cock for a shot.

They were about a third of the way across when a flit of movement at the far edge caused Tom to miss his step and go down on one knee. His knee struck the edge of a large slab and Tom let a short cry slip from his lips as the pain shot up his leg. He dropped the butt of the rifle to the rock to catch himself, fell to his elbow, and from that awkward position, saw a quick glimpse of gold cut through the trees. He was relieved the cat wasn't nearby to take advantage of his position, and slowly worked himself back erect. He moved his hand to his knee to feel it and give himself some comfort and felt the tear in his britches and the blood on his knee that told of his injury. He bent over to take a look and saw it was a bad scrape but not a deep cut, just enough to bring blood. "That's gonna hurt, but can't do anything 'bout it now, can I?" he asked himself quietly. He looked back at Meg that stood patiently and with an expression that told of her disgust with the awkward man and she shook her head up and down as if telling Tom to move along.

He limped across the slide and rounded a large boulder and saw a bed on the lee side of the big rock. The big cat had lain down, and Tom saw a small puddle of blood. As he examined the bed, he could tell the wound was on the cat's rear quarter, but wasn't bleeding enough to be a killing shot, just enough to slow it down. He looked across the rest of the slide trail, saw where the trail entered the trees and figured the cat had stayed to the easier path. "Well, Meg, at least he's movin' slow now, but we gotta keep after him. Can't let him get too far ahead and lose his trail. If he quits bleedin' we might not find him."

Once across the slide rock, Tom mounted Meg and started tracking. With the soft pads and wily ways of the cat, the only giveaway was the drops of blood. Since the cougar had lain down, the blood drops were fewer, but by often checking the trail and other possible routes of escape, Tom was able to stay in pursuit. He continually searched his surroundings, knowing a wounded mountain lion might possibly lay in ambush. As he followed, he tried to remember all he had heard about the ways of the mountain lion, stories from the oldtimers that had confronted the beast in the wild. Some had called them panters or panthers, some called them wildcats, others knew them by the common name of cougar, but all respected them as the most dangerous hunter and killer in the mountains. He had heard stories of old toms too wounded and broken to go after their usual prey of deer and elk and would choose to stalk a man or children. But all told of their crafty ways and silent stalks. Tom searched his environs again, looking for any lofty perch that could be used by the beast to launch his attack.

The trail rounded a large rocky escarpment dotted by a few tenacious piñons that clung to some tiny piece of soil in the cracks of the rock. Tom stood in his stirrups and scanned the slope, seeing nothing, then dropped his eyes to the trail ahead. He held the rifle across the pommel of the saddle, fingers in the lever and thumb on the hammer. Meg bobbed her head and twitched her long ears, snorting her nervousness, but her actions were the same as when they first started trailing the cougar, so Tom was not alarmed. The mule slowed her pace, steps more tenuous, her hoof kicking a rock free to tumble into the trees with only the sound of pine needles ruffled. Tom realized he was holding his breath and started to suck in a lung full when he was suddenly knocked from the saddle, practically over the head of the mule.

The lion rode Tom to the ground, sinking its teeth in his shoulder as Tom squirmed around, still holding his rifle trying to get a shot at his attacker. He felt the fangs tear at his shoulder and the claws of the hind feet of the cougar ripping at his coat, seeking to disembowel the man. The bray of the mule screamed through the trees and suddenly the cat was off. As Tom twisted on the ground, he saw the hooves of the mule striking down and Tom scrambled out of the way as the mule and cat fought. Tom sought to get away and in position for a shot, but the mule switched ends and kicked at the cat with his back hooves just as Tom fired at the cougar. But the beast was sent flying and hit the big boulder with a crunch that Tom knew broke bones, and the cougar fell in a clump into the thin brush below. Meg pranced and brayed threats at the carcass, then looked to the man and dropped her nose to sniff and get her face stroked. Both mule and man were breathing heavy and shaking with both anger and exertion. Tom hugged the mule and spoke softly, reassuring and thanking the faithful mount for saving his life.

He walked over to the brush that held the carcass, pushed some of the branches of the scrub oak aside, and reached with the barrel of the rifle to poke the cat to ensure the animal was dead. There was no movement and Tom stepped closer, looked at the animal that he guessed would measure over ten feet nose to tip of his tail, saw the older scars of battle and the fresh marks from Meg, shook his head and stepped back.

The pain in his shoulder lanced into his consciousness and he unbuttoned his mackinaw to look at the wound. As he pushed back the collar, he saw the blood had already soaked through his union suit and his heavy flannel shirt and he knew he needed to get home to take care of the wound. With who knows what on that cat's claws and teeth, any kind of infection could set in and right quick. He grabbed the reins of the mule, stepped in the stirrup and swung aboard, "Let's go home girl, I gotta get this fixed up a mite."

HE CUT A CORNER FROM THE BEDROLL AND CRAMMED it into his shirt, front and back, attempting to stanch the flow of blood. He didn't want to look too closely at the wound, he already knew by the pain and loss of blood it was worse than he originally thought. But now he had to hold on to get back to the house and Amy, she'd know how to fix him up, sure enough. He gigged Meg to the trail and started through the woods and twisted his head around to look at the sun to gauge the time, knowing it was drawing up on late afternoon.

On the shady side of the slope, the trail bent through some tall timber that held some snow drifts from earlier storms. Meg picked her steps through first one drift then another, none too deep. Just before clearing the timber another drift showed footprints and Tom leaned down for a closer look. He was startled to see the wide tracks of a grizzly, and they had been made that day. He sat up and searched the timber and rocky slope for any movement, fearful of seeing the monster of the mountains while he struggled to stay conscious. He kicked the mule to a trot and then a canter, wanting to be quickly free of the black timber.

By the time Meg reached the corner gate on the upper end of the pasture, Tom was slumped in the saddle, semi-conscious. He lifted his head from Meg's neck, looked at the fence and around, searching for something that he would recognize, but he was unaware he was at his own pasture gate. He drooped in the saddle and started to slide to the side, caught the saddle horn and stopped his movement. He held tightly to the horn and clamped his legs to the pommel to keep from falling, and his mind began to work. He knew he had to open the gate, but if he got down, he didn't think he could get back up in the saddle.

Many times, he had opened gates from atop the saddle, but he thought if he leaned down, he would fall over, but he had to try. He reached for the loop of wire at the top of the gate post, and while he held tight to the horn, he wiggled the wire free and the gate post fell over. But the bottom of the gate post was still in the bottom loop and he couldn't reach it. He dug his heels into the ribs of Meg, trying to get her to step over the downed wire gate, but she danced side to side, resisting.

AMY LEANED TO THE WINDOW, PUSHED THE CURTAIN aside and searched the roadway for the kids. It was about time for them to be home from school and as she leaned side to side to try to see around the cottonwoods that lined the main road, she saw the familiar figures of the children. She dropped the curtain and went to the door, grabbed her coat from the peg and stepped onto the porch to welcome her children home. She stood with arms crossed in front and leaned against the porch post as she waited. She couldn't help herself and turned to look to the far pasture and the tree line for any sign of her husband. She was astonished when she saw the shadowy figure at the corner gate and he seemed to be struggling. It was evident he wasn't sitting tall in the saddle like he usually did, and she tiptoed as if she could see further, but struggled still.

"Hi ma!" came the voice of Tommy, seeing his mother on the porch as usual. It always felt good to see his Mom standing on the porch with a wide smile to welcome the two home. But she didn't wave, instead she was looking the other way, towards the far pasture. His first thought was that another cow was down, and he would have to go look it over like he did the last one. Tammy reached the steps and started up to the porch, Tommy following, when their Mom looked down and the worried expression disappeared as she forced a smile and held her arms wide to welcome her children.

"What is it, Ma, what'd ya see?" asked Tommy, fearful of the answer.

"I think it's your Pa, but you two go inside and get out of your school clothes, I'm going to see if he needs help, now, go on in!" she instructed as she pulled her coat close and started down the steps.

Tommy turned and looked to the pasture, saw Meg by the gate, and watched as the mule picked her steps through the downed wire gate. His Ma was running as best she could and was already nearing the bridge.

"C'mon Tommy, Momma said!" whined Tammy as she tugged at his coat.

"You go ahead, Tammy, Ma and Pa might need my help. Go on now," he instructed as he turned to watch the goings on in the pasture. He watched as his Ma met Meg, caught up the reins and reached to the still form on the saddle. He could tell his Pa must be hurt or something to be laying over the pommel that way. He saw his Ma hold onto the headstall and lead the mule over the bridge and Tommy ran to the near gate to open it for them.

"What's wrong Ma? What happened?" asked the boy.

"I don't know, Tommy. But your father is hurt pretty bad and he can't tell me. You need to help me get him into the house, and then you might have to go to town to get the doctor."

Tommy held the gate open for his Ma to lead the mule through, closed it and followed her to the porch. She led the mule beside the steps and dropped the reins to ground tie her, stepped back and standing on the second step reached for her husband. Tommy stood closer to the mule and reached up to help his dad down. It was all the two could do, but they finally managed to get him inside and on the bed. Tommy stood and watched his mother struggle with the heavy Mackinaw coat, and she turned to Tommy for help.

"I'm going to push him up, you hold him there and I'll pull his clothes off this side, and we'll have to do it again for the other side. Understand?"

"Yeah, Ma, I understand."

When they saw the blood, both Tommy and his Ma gasped, but Amy steeled herself and continued. She stopped and turned to the boy, "Tommy, you take Meg and get to town and tell the doctor we need him right away. It looks like your Pa got jumped by a mountain lion or something, now hurry!"

"Yes'm, I'll hurry. We'll be right back, I promise!"

He ran from the house and jumped from the steps to the saddle, leaned down and reached beside the mule's neck and grabbed the reins. Tommy pulled her head around and slapped leather, "C'mon Meg, we gotta get to town and get the doctor! Pa's hurt bad!"

DUSK WAS DROPPING THE CURTAIN ON THE LIGHT OF day when Tommy came running up the roadway astride the big mule. Right behind came the doctor in his one seat buggy behind the high stepping black gelding with four white stocking legs. The doctor was proud of his buggy and the horse but not so much for its beauty but because of its stamina and speed, qualities needed in a doctor's horse. Dr. Spradley reined up at the steps and Tommy said, "Go on in Doc, I'll take care of your horse."

The doctor stepped from the buggy, bag in hand and took the steps two at a time. The door opened as he reached for it and Amy said, "Oh doctor, thanks for coming so soon," she turned to lead him to the bedroom, "it looks bad, doctor, awful bad."

"What happened Amy, the boy said a lion or a bear?"

"Yes, we had a cow killed and he went after whatever killed it. But when he came back, he was barely conscious and couldn't tell me. It looks like claw and teeth marks, and if it wasn't for that heavy Mackinaw coat, it would'a been a lot worse."

TOMMY SAT WITH TAMMY AT THE TABLE, HOLDING THE girl's hand, as they waited. His mom would come from the bedroom with an arm full of bloody cloths, get another bunch and grab the teapot with hot water, and disappear back in the room, and then do it all over again. This last time, she left the teapot and asked, "Could you fill that up with water and stoke up the stove please?"

"Sure Ma. Ma, is he going to be alright?"

"Of course, honey, he'll be fine, it's just going to take a while and we'll have to take care of him. The doctor's fixing him up real fine. Don't worry." She disappeared into the bedroom again.

Tommy remembered they had not had supper and he looked around to see what his mom had been preparing. On the back of the stove was a big cast iron pot, lid still on, and he went to see what it held. Using one of his Mom's pot-holders, he lifted the lid and steam wafted up with the smells of a pot roast. He looked at the meat, potatoes, onions, and carrots, took a deep breath and said to Tammy, "Here's supper. Get us some plates an' I'll dish us up some."

THE BEDROOM DOOR OPENED AND BOTH AMY AND THE doctor came out, the doctor rolling his sleeves down as Amy toted his bag. "Won't you stay for supper doctor? I've got a nice pot roast we'd be pleased to share with you."

"Well, that sounds mighty fine, Mrs. Turner. I'll have to admit, I've been smelling it and my stomach has been growling for it."

Amy smiled and set his bag down beside the divan, went back to the kitchen area to prepare things for the doctor. The doctor took a seat at the table, looked to the children and said, "Looks like these two couldn't wait any longer."

Amy looked at her children, smiled and said, "Well, I've tried to teach them to be self-sufficient. So, you two, did you save enough for us?"

"Sure Ma, we couldn't eat it all. We're just kids!" declared Tammy.

Tommy looked to the doctor and asked, "Is Pa gonna be alright?"

"Sure, he is, he's a big strong man and he's not going to let a little mountain lion do him in, no sir."

Tommy smiled at the doctor, "So, it was a mountain lion?"

"That's what he said. He also said he killed it too."

Tommy smiled at the thought of his Pa killing the mountain lion and wished he could have been with him. But he was just relieved and happy his Pa was going to be alright. He remembered his Pa telling him that he should always be thankful to the Lord for answered prayer and Tommy had prayed all the way to town and back. He bowed his head and said a silent prayer of thanks, grateful for all the Lord had done for them.

"Now remember, he needs plenty of rest, change those bandages regular, and liquids and red meat. He's lost a lot of blood and that's what it's going to take to build it back up. And, don't forget, keep those wounds clean and if there's any sign of infection, you send for me, right away, y'hear?"

"Yes, doctor. And thank you so much for coming out. I'll do as you say," answered a contrite Amy, she had started to scold Tom and was stopped by the doctor.

"He might be in and out of consciousness for a spell, but that's normal after such a tussle as he had with that mountain lion. It took a lot out of him, not just blood, mind you. But I'm sure, in time, he'll be alright."

"He's going to be wanting to get back to work," started Amy, questioning the doctor.

"I know, I know, this time of year and all, but he'll need at least a couple days rest before he even thinks about it, but if you tell him I said he needs to take a week, maybe he'll compromise with two or three days," suggested Dr. Spradley, grinning conspiratorially. "you know how some of these men are, don't you?"

Amy dropped her head, nodding agreement, "Yes I do! And sometimes this one is the worst of the lot. Trying to get him to even slow down is like grabbing a bull by the horns."

"Well, I'll check on him in about a week, unless you send for me." He doffed his hat and opened the door to leave.

"Thanks again, Doctor."

Tommy had fetched the doctor's horse and buggy and led the horse to the steps. "You're sure he's gonna be alright, Doc?"

"Yes, Tommy. He'll need some rest and care, but I'm sure he'll be fine. Thanks for tending to my horse and bringing him up. You're a good boy."

Tommy just nodded his head as he mounted the steps to the porch, turning to watch the doctor drive away. He was thinking about his Pa and how they were going to keep him abed and resting, what with the banker worrying him and all. He shook his head, once again, wondering what he could do to help. He had done his chores while the doctor worked on his Pa and he was tired, thinking about his bed in the loft when he stepped into the house and saw his mother at the table, head in her hands.

"What's the matter, Ma? Is it Pa? Is he alright?" asked Tommy in borderline panic as he looked toward the bedroom door. His mother lifted her head and he saw tear-filled eyes above a forced smile as she reached for his hand, using the other hand to daub at her tears.

"He's alright, Tommy, he's alright. I guess it's just tears of relief, he had me scared there for a while, but the doctor said he's going to be fine. You don't need to worry your little head about it. Now, you get ready for bed, Tammy's already turned in and you need to also."

"Are you sure, Ma, I mean, are you sure Pa's gonna be alright?" pleaded the boy.

"Yes, I'm sure. We're just going to have to make sure he gets lots of rest and the doctor said he'll need red meat to help build up his blood. So, that's what we'll do," she explained, nodding her head.

Tommy looked at his Ma, thought about what she said and answered, "But Ma, we ain't got no red meat. We had the last of that quarter we had hangin' an' all you got in the cellar is what you canned."

Her eyes widened as she considered what the boy said, thought about it as she looked around the counters and cupboards from where she sat and looked back at Tommy. "We'll think of something, Tommy. In the meantime, you get to bed. You've got school tomorrow and there's going to be a rehearsal for the Christmas play. Have you studied your lines?"

"A little, it ain't much anyway. But I'll get it," answered a tired boy who was wishing he was a man about now. Maybe then he could help his Ma take care of Pa. He dropped his head and started for his loft.

"Wait just a minute young man! You better not think about going to bed without giving your mother a kiss good-night," she scolded, smiling and holding out her arms. Tommy ran back to his mother's embrace and after a kiss and a hug that made him feel so much better, he started for his bed in the loft.

Tommy explained to Mrs. Davis and Mrs. Leggitt why his mother could not be there for the practice but that she promised she would be there for the practice later in the week. Both ladies understood and told Tommy they would be in prayer for his folks and then everyone set about to have a good practice for the program. It wasn't over soon enough for Tommy but as soon as it was, he and Tammy and their neighbors started for home.

When Cody asked about his Pa and the mountain lion, Tommy quickly answered, "Yeah, that lion got ahold o' Pa, but Pa kilt him. Kilt him deader'n a doornail!"

"Did he bring back the hide?"

"Nah, he was loosin' blood an' needed to get home. We'll prob'ly go get the hide later. Ain't no varmints gonna be pickin' at a cougar's carcass, anyway," bragged Tommy.

"Boy, that's really sumpin' Tommy, your Pa killin' a cougar, I mean," declared Clarissa, smiling at Tommy. She had always thought of Tommy as the boy that would be her boyfriend, if she had one, that is, but she never told him. Now she walked beside him, occasionally touching shoulders as they walked.

"Yeah, I guess so, but that didn't surprise me none. My Pa was a hero in the war, ya' know," he declared, puffing out his chest a bit as he fumbled with the strap holding his books and slate over his shoulder.

"Really?" she responded, eyes wide and wondering.

"Yup, got him some medals an' all. Don't rightly know what he did cuz he won't talk about it, but they don't give medals for nothin' ya' know."

"Gosh! That's somethin'," answered an amazed fourth grade girl with eyes full of curiosity.

"Well, see ya' tomorrow!" declared Tommy as he reached for Tammy's hand and nodding to his friends as they started down their road. Cody and Clarissa waved back at their friends and turned away. Tommy looked to his sister and said, "We gotta hurry a bit, sis. We've gotta get our chores done and see if we can help Ma with Pa. We might have to fix our own supper cuz she has to nurse Pa all day."

"Pa's gonna be alright, ain't he?" asked a timid voice coming from a fearful seven-year-old little sister.

"Sure, he is, Doc said so, and Doc knows what he's doin' silly. Now come on, let's get home."

Amy had taken up her vigil in a rocking chair beside their bed. She sat quietly, rocking absentmindedly, as she sewed on the costumes for the children and the Christmas play. Tommy's costume was simple enough, he was to be the Innkeeper. But Tammy was to be the angel and hers required a bit more attention. But all the while she sewed, she kept thinking about what they would do for Tom to have red meat and now with these days off work, how could they make the payment to the bank. But answers were not forthcoming and after sticking herself with the needle for the third time, she sat the sewing aside and picked up the book beside her, *A Christmas Carol in Prose, by Charles Dickens.* She had read it before, but it had been several years ago and now just wanted something to clear her mind, yet she found herself comparing Ebenezer Scrooge to J.B. Randall and their own predicament with the bank. She shook her head and sat the book back on the small table at her side and reached for the cloth in the basin.

She wrung out the cloth and stood to wipe Tom's forehead, and his eyes fluttered open. She wiped his brow and he smiled and reached for her hand, "How long have I been asleep?"

"This time, just a couple of hours, but you need to rest," she answered, sitting back in her chair, arm stretched out as she held his hand. "Are you ready for some more broth? I'll heat it back up," she offered.

He struggled to sit up, wincing at the discomfort of his shoulder and upper arm, and grabbed at it as it pained him. He lifted his eyes back to his wife and nodded his head as he twisted around to drop his legs over the side of the bed. She nodded, knowing he needed a moment of privacy to tend to his needs, and left the room, pulling the door shut behind her. At the stove, she checked the burner for warmth, slid it open and dropped in a couple of pieces of wood, and sat the pan with the broth back on the burner. She went to the window and looked to the corral at the horses and mule and in the distance at the cattle in the pasture, remembering the downed cow that started all this, hoping that it wouldn't happen again. She heard the pot rattle on the burner as the broth started to move and stepped back to the stove. With a potholder in hand, she lifted the pot from the stove, closed the damper on the stove, and started back to the bedroom. Tom had just seated himself on the edge of the bed and looked up as she entered.

"Whew! I'm weaker'n I thought," he mumbled as he lifted his legs back to the bed as he lay back on the pillows, "an' I never thought broth could taste so good, but I'm both hungry and thirsty so it'll be just fine."

Amy smiled as she sat the pot down on the trivet atop the small table. She pulled the chair a little closer and dipped the ladle into the broth, holding a cloth in her hand underneath, and held it to her husband's lips. He slurped it noisily and greedily, licking his lips after every spoonful and smiling his gratitude at his wife. She laughed at his manners and said, "I guess I'm going to have to fix you something more substantial, you reckon?"

"Sounds might fine to me. With nothin' but this broth, I'm gettin' so hungry, my belly button's pinchin' my backbone!" he declared.

Amy giggled at his expression, holding her free hand with the cloth to her mouth and answered, "Well, at least you're sounding better. For a while there, all you were doing was squeaking like a mouse and I could hardly make out what you were saying."

"That's cuz I wanted you to lean close enough for a kiss, but you just kept sayin' 'what?' 'what?' and you weren't gettin' the drift of what I was tryin' for, so I just gave up," he explained, rolling his eyes.

"Oh, now I know you're doing better, that mischievousness is coming out. So, you'll just have to excuse me while I start our supper. The children will be home soon and I'm sure they'll be hungry also."

IT WAS WELL BEFORE DAYLIGHT AND AFTER TOSSING and turning for a long while, Tom rolled out of bed. He grabbed his pants hanging from the bedstead and slipped them on. His shoulder and upper arm still gave him pain and he knew they would for quite a while, but he just couldn't stand lying in bed all day long and then be unable to sleep at night. He tried to be quiet and not disturb Amy, but she rolled to her side and asked, "What are you doing?"

"I can't sleep, I've got to move around before I go crazy! I've spent almost three days in this bed and I just can't sleep anymore. I'm just restless, I guess, go on back to sleep, I'll be fine. I might go out to the barn and check on stuff for the props the Pastor's wantin', or somethin'. Anything besides layin' in bed."

They were speaking in soft tones, but Tommy heard the movement and stirred but did not come fully awake and the creak of his bed made Amy "shush" Tom and he nodded his head. He whispered, "I know, I know, I'll be quiet. You go back to sleep now." He tiptoed out of the bedroom, went to the stove and stoked it up before he slid the half empty coffee pot onto the burner plate. Once it was warm enough, Tom poured himself a steaming cup full, slipped on his Mackinaw, patched up and repaired by Amy, and slipped through the door.

The full moon hung in the darkness, dwarfing the lesser lights of the stars. Tom looked up to see it was a clear night and cold, but the chill air felt good on his face. He rubbed his mittened hands on his arms and shoulders as he walked to the barn. He slid the door back and stepped into the darkness. The glow of the moon filtered through the doorway, giving just enough light for him to find the kerosene lantern hanging from the usual peg. He tucked a mitten under his arm, dug for a lucifer in his coat pocket, lifted his leg and drug the lucifer the length of his thigh on his canvas britches and as it sprung to flame he lifted the chimney on the lantern and lit the wick. The smell of sulfur mingled with the usual barn smells and Tom drew deep on these pungent odors of ranch life. He grinned as he slipped the other mitten back on and walked to the workbench along the far wall.

The dim light of the lantern showed the stack of rejected lodgepole timbers that Tom expected to use to build the manger setting for the church. The skinny poles had been the smallest of his harvest in the spring upon his return, meant for poles for the corrals, but proved too small to use to hold either horses or cows. But they would be just the right size and light enough to use to fashion the manger setting.

He busied himself thinking about a plan or design for the manger, using a piece of charcoal to scratch a rough drawing on the work bench. He looked at his drawing, down at the poles, and made a few changes. When he was satisfied with his plan, he started laying out the poles, one-handed and sparing his wounded wing but in enough of a lay-out that he could begin putting them together. He planned to use a brace and bit and pegs to do the job but would also have to use some twine to reinforce the joints. He also needed to make it in pieces, so it could be hauled in the wagon and assembled at the church.

"Hey Pa! Whatcha doin'?" asked Tommy, startling his Pa who was focused on his job.

Tom lifted his head and was surprised to see the first grey light of dawn coming through the now open barn door, thanks to Tommy, and the smiling face of his son peering out from under the brim of his fur lined cap. "Oh, I guess I lost track of the time. I couldn't sleep, and I thought I'd get started on the Pastor's sets for the Christmas program." He had been sitting on the ground and working away with his brace and bit and now set the tool aside and stood to stretch his legs. Looking at Tommy he said, "You're up an' at 'em early this mornin'," grinning at his son carrying an empty milk pail.

"Nah, not really," he hung the pail by its bail on a post, reached for the pitchfork and headed for the hay mow. Tom watched the boy methodically go through his routine of feeding the animals, checking their water, and turn to the chore of milking old Bossy, their Guernsey milk cow.

"Well, it looks like you got things well in hand, so I'm going back inside. I think I'll try to go to work today, so maybe I can give you a ride to school. How 'bout that?" he asked.

"Suits me. That'll give me a little more time for breakfast an' I'm mighty hungry."

Tom smiled at his son and started for the house. He was proud of his boy and knew he was growing up all too fast. But he was confident Tommy would grow into a fine man.

He had always been diligent about his chores, seldom griping, and always doing a good job. No man could be prouder of a son than was Tom. He looked back over his shoulder to the barn door and the boy within.

As Tom stepped into the house, slipping from his coat, he saw the wide smile of Amy standing near the stove as she greeted him, "Well, it's about time. And you timed it just right. The biscuits are coming out of the oven and the sausage gravy is about done. Come and get these eggs and put them on the table, please."

Tom was glad to oblige because he knew he could steal a kiss when he picked up the platter of eggs, and he didn't even have to steal it. Amy freely offered his reward and topped it off with a giggle and a smile.

"Eeewww, do you have to do that all the time?" came a tiny voice from the table.

"Yes, we do!" declared her father as he sat the platter of eggs on the table, then bent to his daughter, "And we do too!" he declared as he kissed Tammy who answered with her own giggles. He put the tip of his finger on the tip of her nose and added, "And you're just like your mother, kisses and giggles!"

The wind chased Tommy as he opened the door and stumbled in, straddling the milk pail as it sloshed the milk about. He kicked the door closed and set the bucket down to take off his coat and cap. He took his place at the table just as his mother set the bowl of gravy and basket of biscuits down. When she sat down, she stretched out her hands and the family joined hands as Tom led them in prayer. He thanked the Lord for his protection, for his healing, and for his family and the fine meal. When he finished, they said "Amen" together and started their meal.

When Tommy asked for seconds on the biscuits and

gravy, his Ma asked, "Will you have time? You've got to get to school."

"Sure Ma. Pa said he was going to work and would give us a ride, so I got plenty of time."

Amy looked at Tom with eyes wide, questioning her husband. "Don't you remember what the Doctor said?"

"Yes, I know. But I'm feelin' pretty good and I'm sure I can at least work a half a day, maybe more. Ol' Jasper knows I can't do too much, but I'm sure I can be a help, an' I know they're gettin' backed up, what with that order for ties from the railroad."

"Oh, and I suppose you think you can go throwing railroad ties around with that arm?"

"No, I'm not even gonna try that. But there's other things I can do and if I get wore out, I'll come home. But you know we need the money."

Amy dropped her eyes and nodded, "Yes, I know. But I need you more than we need the money."

Tom knew he couldn't answer that statement and chose to copy his son and reach for another biscuit. He looked at Tommy, "Even though you're getting a ride, I will need your help puttin' the harness on them horses. So, we need to get a move on, alright?"

"Sure Pa," answered the boy, between bites, but smiling all the same.

THE RIDE INTO TOWN WAS QUIET. THE COOL AIR KEPT the children huddled under the blanket beside their Pa, but Tommy kept looking at his Pa, noticing how he held his left arm close in and handled the reins one handed. He had seen the claw marks and teeth punctures when his Ma changed the bandages and he was amazed at how much damage was done and how his Pa was able to even move his arm. His shoulder had been ripped open front and back and the teeth had dug into the upper arm and even torn that back. He knew it had to hurt but he also knew not to say anything, it was just the way men dealt with things, you don't talk about it, you just go about your business. But as Tommy looked again at his Pa and saw him struggling with the pain, he vowed to pray for him even more than before.

And he had to think of some way he could help with everything, everything that was bothering his Ma and Pa. Surely there was something. All day long while the teacher talked or passed out assignments, Tommy was thinking about what he could do, and a plan began to take shape. He knew the family needed meat and especially his Pa needed more red meat, even if he was going back to work. Just this morning, he had seen a couple of deer by the willows beside Little River. He hadn't paid much attention at the time, but now he began to think about them. It was not unusual to see deer there early in the morning and early evening when they came to water. And if he watched to see exactly where they were, they probably had beds in those willows, then maybe he could get to them and get one of them with his rifle. His plan was shaping up and he smiled to himself, thinking this was going to be the way he could help.

"So, STUDENTS, THE SHORTEST DAY AND LONGEST NIGHT of the year is the time that is called...?" tested Mrs. Parks, waiting for an answer.

"Winter Solstice," answered the class in unison.

"Very good! Now, don't concern yourselves, it will not be on your next test. It's just good information for you to know." She looked at the clock on the wall and added, "It's almost time to be dismissed. Now, all of you that are a part of the Community Church program, don't forget you have a practice at the church just after school." She walked back to her desk and turned around to look at the classroom full of students, "And remember, after the weekend, we only have three more days of school until you're dismissed for our Christmas vacation, so be sure to do your best as you study for the term tests. Now, please stand," she watched as the children stood to their feet beside their desks, smiling anxiously at the close of the school day. "You're dismissed." The youngsters gathered their books and slates, most tying them together with a belt or twine for carrying and filed to the foyer to get their coats and caps.

. . .

THE PROGRAM PRACTICE QUICKLY GOT UNDERWAY AND
Tommy and Eleanor took their places as the Innkeeper and
his wife. Tommy imitated opening the door of the Inn and
after waiting for Cody to rehearse his lines, Tommy scowled
and answered, "No, we have no room in the Inn." He turned
as Eleanor tugged on his sleeve and suggested, "Maybe they
could stay in the manger? After all, she is expecting a baby
and they need someplace warm."

"Very good, children. Now, Tommy, you are to point to
the other side of the platform where the manger will be, and
you'll follow Joseph and Mary to the manger," directed the
pastor's wife, Rebekah. The rest of the practice went very
well and the director, Rebekah Davis, said, "Now, before
you're dismissed, let me remind you to practice your lines,
practice, practice, practice. We only have one week before
Christmas Eve and our program, and we only have two
more rehearsals, so do your best and practice." She smiled at
each of the children, nodded her head and said, "Thank you
for being here and working so hard. Now, go home and have
a good week-end."

As the children filed out of the church, Tommy was
surprised to see his Pa sitting on their wagon, grinning and
apparently waiting for them. He ran to the wagon and
asked, "Pa, what're you doin' here?"

"Well, I thought I'd give you and your sister and Ma a
ride home, is that alright? If not, I'll go ahead and wait for
you at home," and he made like he was picking up the reins
to start off without them, grinning all the while.

"No, no! Don't go! Sure, we want a ride!" He turned as
Tammy tugged at his sleeve and helped her up to put her
foot on the hub of the wheel and then to the side step to

make it into the wagon. He started to climb up but was stopped by his Pa, "Whoa there, wait for your Ma and help her too, son." He turned to look for his Ma, saw her coming through the door and hollered, "Hey Ma! Pa's here to give us a ride!"

She waved as she came down the steps and was quickly to the side of the wagon. She accepted the hand of her son to help her to the step and reached for her husband's hand with the other and was soon seated beside her man. Tommy clambered up and settled in beside his sister, covering up their legs with the quilt and even pulling the quilt up to their chins. When Tom saw the twins start up the road, he spoke up and said, "C'mon Cody and Clarissa, climb on up and we'll drop you off at your road."

Two smiling faces soon settled in beside Tommy and Tammy and the friends shared the warm quilt. Cody leaned around his sister, who had seated herself beside Tommy, and asked, "So, are you still goin' huntin' tomorrow?" Tommy shushed him, looking up at the back of his Pa to see if he had heard, but the creaking of the wagon, the rattle of trace chains and the conversation of the adults kept them from hearing the question of Cody. Tommy leaned over and whispered almost into Cody's ear, "Nobody's supposed to know. It's a Christmas surprise and my Pa doesn't want Ma to know about it." Cody nodded his understanding and looked up at the adults to see if they were listening.

Tom and Amy huddled close together, with Amy putting her hand through the crook of Tom's elbow and leaning her head on his shoulder. Tom looked to the clouds in the fading light, "Those clouds are looking like we might get a storm tonight," he observed, nodding in the direction of the clouds hanging over the mountains on the south edge of the valley. "Can't even see the top of Mt. Ouray, and the temperature seems to be dropping awful fast, yup, I'm thinkin' we'll see snow come mornin'," declared Tom.

"Well good, I was hoping for a white Christmas. It's just not the same when there's no snow, don't you think?"

"Well, snow does make it mighty pretty, long as it ain't too much! It can be hard on the cattle when it gets too deep for them to paw down to the grass and we don't have enough hay in the barn to do too much feedin'."

Tommy was listening to his folks talk about the snow and he was thinking about his plan to go after a deer. He remembered his Pa often talking about how a little snow helps when you're hunting, it's easier to track the deer and they don't move around as much. He smiled, thinking it would be good if they got some snow tonight, it would prob-ably make it better for his plan.

"Oh, and I meant to tell you, I have another piano student! Rebekah wants to take lessons too! And she wants to start tomorrow, right after Eleanor!" declared Amy as she hugged Tom's arm.

Tom looked down at his wife and answered, "That's good, I guess. But if we get too much snow, it might be hard to walk home."

"Oh, I'm not worried. You'll take me in and if it's too deep to walk, I'm sure the Pastor will bring me home with his buggy. Rebekah said she loves to go out in the snow," commented Amy, giggling a little, then turned her head to her husband, "she even thought it would be fun if they had to borrow a sleigh to get around." Tom just shook his head at how some would think of how fun a heavy snowstorm could be while others worried about how it could be so devas-tating and destructive.

They dropped the twins off at their roadway and were soon at home with the wagon stopped by the steps. Tom jumped down and helped his wife down, then the children and Amy instructed the two, "Alright, now hurry and get out of your school clothes and get to your chores. It will be dark real soon and it's hard to find eggs in the dark!" she said as she looked at Tammy with a smile. The two youngsters were soon back outside and beginning their chores as Tom finished unharnessing the horses and putting them in their stalls.

Tom headed for the house, joining hands with Tammy as she carried the basket of freshly gathered eggs. Tommy was finishing up with forking the hay and watched his dad and sister go to the house. Once they were inside, Tommy went to the back door of the barn and looked out at the pasture with the Little River running through the middle with its clusters of willows and the rare cottonwood tree. He was searching for any sign of deer, the deer he planned on hunting in the morning. As he thought about his plan, he smiled thinking about how pleased his mother would be when he brought home some fresh venison. The way he thought it out, after his Ma and Pa left in the morning, Ma to the piano lessons and his Pa to his usual work at the mill, he would have most of the morning to go to the willows, find the deer in their beds, take one with the .22, field dress it and get the mule to pack it back to the house. By the time his Ma came back home after the piano lessons, he would have the fresh haunch of deer on the table and the rest hanging in the cellar. He chuckled to himself about what a great Christmas it would be with all that fresh meat and one less thing for his folks to worry about.

He shut the barn door, stuck the pitchfork in the hay pile and stepped off toward the house. He thought of what his Pa would often say, *Yessir, son, when you have a good plan about what you're gonna do, why, the job's almost as good as done. At least the doin' of it's a sight easier and when you're done, there's a certain pride a man can have when the job's done and done right.* He had a jaunty bounce to his step as he reached the stairs to the porch and took then two at a time. He was anxious for the morning, so he could put his plan into action.

Tommy's excitement and anticipation rolled him out of bed just as soon as he heard movement below. When he heard his Pa say they had fresh snow, he made sure to put on his wool union suit under his heavy corduroy britches and heavy flannel shirt. He laced up his Buster Brown high topped shoes over his wool socks that were knitted by his mom, stood and stomped his feet, thinking he would be warm in the coldest weather. He descended the ladder to the room below and was greeted by his Pa as he sat down for breakfast.

"So, you're up early on this Saturday morning!"

"Ah Pa, you know Bossy don't know what day it is, an' if'n I wait till too late, she gets troublesome when I try to milk her!" he answered, thinking of the temperamental Guernsey. She was known to be less than cooperative if she was made to wait too long for her breakfast of grain and the relief of her full bag. His Pa explained that when the bag gets full of milk, if the cow doesn't get relief, it begins to pain her, and she gets temperamental. The last thing

Tommy wanted to do this morning was fight with an unpredictable milk cow.

"Well, c'mon and have your breakfast. She won't mind, since you're so early this mornin'," suggested his Pa as he pulled out a chair for his son. As Tommy seated himself, his Pa continued, "I'm gonna try to come home a little early today, so maybe you can give me a hand with the makin' of those sets for the Pastor and the Christmas program, what say?"

"Sure Pa, be glad too. Pass the biscuits, please."

"Whoa up there pardner, we need to pray 'bout it first," directed his Pa. Amy came to the table to hold hands with her men and Tom led them in a short prayer of thanks and asked for the Lord's hand in everything that was needed for the day. Once the "Amen" was said, Tommy wasted little time finishing his breakfast and excusing himself to go to his chores.

Once he was bundled up, milk pail in hand, he started for the door but was stopped by his Ma. "We'll probably be gone when you're done milking, and I want you to take care of your sister while we're gone. I'll probably be home about noon time, so, I'm counting on you to take care while we're gone, understand?"

"Sure Ma, I understand." He ducked his head, thinking about his plan and felt a little guilty but he was certain that Tammy would be fine in the house by herself for the short while when he went after the deer. He would make sure everything was just right before he left, and he would explain it to Tammy and he was certain she would be willing to be a part of his plan. As he opened the door, he waved at his folks and disappeared into the cool of the morning.

He was surprised to see the wagon and team already

standing at the foot of the stairs but realized his Pa had apparently risen earlier than he thought and knew the movement in the house that woke him was when his Pa came back into the house after hitching the team. He walked around the wagon and ducked his head into the wind and snow and went to the barn. The storm had brought a couple of inches of fresh snow and was still shaking the trees as it dropped more snow. It had more wind than snow and it seemed the snow was going more horizontal than laying down to accumulate. It wasn't what would be called a blizzard, but it was certainly cold, and it was difficult to see very far.

Once in the barn, he pulled the main door shut to keep out the wind but went to the back door to survey the pasture for his quarry. He didn't really expect to see any deer, as his Pa had often told him that the deer would bed down out of the wind whenever a storm came, but maybe he could catch one moving around by their beds. He squinted his eyes and with his hand at his forehead to shield them, he searched the reaches of the pasture, but nothing stirred but the storm. His hopes were still high when he turned back to his task of forking the hay and milking the cow.

He was just exiting the barn when he heard his Pa slap the horses on their rumps with the reins and the creak of the wagon and the crunch of the fresh snow under the big wheels told him they were on their way. He quickened his pace and mounted the steps just as Tammy opened the door for him and stepped aside as he entered. Sitting the pail down, he took off his cap and scarf, undid his coat and stomped his feet.

"Thanks sis, you're great!" and he bent to pick up the pail and set it on the counter. He turned to Tammy and said, "Let's sit at the table, I got somethin' to tell you." When they were seated, Tommy took his sister's hand in his and began, "You know how we've talked a little 'bout how Ma and Pa have been worried about things, you know, the bank and stuff. Well, I've been trying to think of some way we could help, and I think I've found a way."

"Really? Good, what can I do?" asked the eager girl.

"Well, here's my plan..." and he began to explain all about trying to get a deer and help with the family's need for fresh meat. "And what you will need to do is to stay here in the house by yourself, and keep the stove going so it'll be warm when I get back. Now, I'm only goin' to be out there in the pasture, and if'n I get a deer right away, I shouldn't be gone long. I'm gonna stoke up the stove and ever'thing, so you won't have to do much. And lookee here," he reached under his small pack on the table and pulled out a thin book and pushed it toward her. "I got this from the library for you," and showed her the book, *Campfire Girls on a Hike, or Lost in the Great North Woods, by Stella M. Francis.*

Tammy's eyes lit up, "Oh Tommy, thank you! It sounds like a great book!" Tommy knew his sister loved to read and had an ability far exceeding her years that was a thirst for knowledge that was seldom slaked. She looked at her brother, "So, my part will be to just stay here and keep the house warm while you're out there in the snow trying to get a deer?"

"Uh huh, that's right. Ma will be back by about noon, and I should be back before then. You think you'll be alright?"

"Sure, and with this good book to read, I probably won't even miss you!" she declared as she smiled at her big brother.

"That's great sis, and when I get the deer, it'll be our present for the folks and one less thing for them to worry about," he declared as he stood to finish his preparations for his hunt. His pack was just a draw string bag big enough for a few items. He had his Pa's hunting knife and scabbard, an extra scarf, and several biscuits well lathered with apple butter and wrapped in a dishtowel his Ma had made from an old flour sack. He had a couple more biscuits in the pocket of his coat, not that he expected to need them, but his favorite food was his Ma's biscuits and apple butter and any excuse to partake was not overlooked by Tommy. He also had some twine just in case he needed to tie up the carcass or had to drag it a ways, his Pa's flint and steel and some tinder was wrapped in a piece of buckskin, and he couldn't think of anything else he would need so he drew the bag's string tight and went to the rack to take down the .22 rifle. He checked to make sure it was loaded by drawing the slide or pump back that opened the chamber. He jacked in a cartridge, pulled the pump back in place and lowered the hammer, put the rifle on safety and lay it on the table. He put a couple of hands full of cartridges in his coat pocket, the one opposite his biscuits and looked around to make sure he wasn't forgetting anything.

He was bundled up, coat, scarf, cap, mittens, pack and stood at the door, "Alright sis, I'm headed for the willows and gonna get that deer. You enjoy your book and I should be back soon."

She sat still at the table and waved at her brother as he stepped out the door. When the door shut out the cold air the house was silent, and the girl looked around and felt so alone. The wood crackled in the flames as the logs fell, the window over the counter rattled as the cold wind of the winter storm rapped on the pane. She listened to every sound, none unfamiliar, but each with its own reminder that she was all alone. She grabbed the book and slid off the chair and went to the rocker nearer the stove. Ma's knitted afghan smelled of her mother and Tammy sat on the rocker, her feet not touching the floor and she slid down, pushed the footstool nearer and climbed back into the rocker. She stretched the afghan over her legs, pushed against the footstool and started the chair into a gently rocking motion and she leaned back, looked at the cover of her book, smiled and turned to the first page, determined to lose herself in the story and escape from this loneliness.

Tommy chose to walk through the barn instead of wrestling with the wire gate. This would give him a better route to the willows and he could follow the brush upstream, watching for the deer and hopefully get one before it saw him. He ducked his head against the wind, mindful of the direction it was blowing and knew he had to have the wind at his face to keep the deer from getting his scent and scattering. Once he reached the willows, he paused, enjoying the temporary respite from the storm with the willows as a windbreak. He had the .22 cradled in his arms and looked at the safety and the hammer, knowing he had to be ready to release the safety, the button near the trigger, and bring the hammer to a full cock, before he could shoot the rifle. He thought about his movements and was confident he would do it right. He dropped to one knee, pulled his scarf up over his nose to shield his chin and cheeks, pulled his cap down so only his eyes were unencumbered, and searched the willows. He watched for just a couple of moments and started his slow walk, scanning the brush for any movement or form. He knew he might only see the twitch of an ear or less as the deer were hunkered down to wait out the storm and the chances of one jumping up in front of him were slim.

He moved slowly, one step, pause, two steps pause and

search the brush, another step and look. He had moved a little more than thirty yards, slowly and quietly, when a slight movement made him pause in his steps and move his head only a little to try to identify what it was that caught his sight. His Pa had told him that he would usually see something only because it moved and usually when you weren't looking directly at it, so he slowly scanned the brush. There! The shadowy outline of the head and big ears of a deer. Now he cautiously turned to look directly at the deer, pushing the safety off and quietly bringing the hammer to a full cock. Suddenly the deer sprung to its feet, looked directly at Tommy to identify its threat, and just as the spike buck turned to flee, Tommy raised the rifle to his shoulder and drew a bead.

The young buck turned toward the stream and jumped like he had springs for legs, the sudden movement startling Tommy and making him pull the trigger in his excitement. He saw the buck flinch, and he pumped another shell in for a second shot as the buck made two quick hops and crossed the river and disappeared into the brush on the opposite bank. Tommy looked, knew he had to use the bridge to cross and ran to the bridge less than ten yards away. He quickly crossed over, forgetting the storm and with adrenalin driving him on, he ran to the point of the willows where the buck had crossed the stream, all the while searching for any sign of the deer running across the field. He easily spotted the tracks of the buck where it came from the willows and he dropped to his knees to look closely at the sign. He rose to follow the tracks, watching carefully for any sign of blood that would indicate he had scored a hit. Within just a few steps, he saw the bright red droplets where the warm blood showed in the fresh white snow. He smiled at the thought he had made a successful shot, but then he realized what was in store. His Pa had often said that whenever you hit an animal with a shot, you have to track it down to make sure you get the game. It's not right to wound an animal and let it die a miserable death and lay to rot in the woods. Besides, the whole idea was to get the meat for his family. He looked back to the house, barely visible in the white of the storm, and down at the tracks. He followed the tracks with his eyes and knew the trail would lead to the woods beyond the edge of the pasture. He thought just a moment at the task before him and shrugged his shoulders and started for the woods, head bowed before the blowing snow, hoping he would find the deer before the storm got too bad.

He wasn't prepared for an extended hunt and he knew a winter storm showed no mercy no matter that he was a nine-year-old, going on ten, and headed into the woods. He would just have to do what's right and make sure he got the deer before it was too late. After all, that's what a man would do, and this was a man's job he had tackled. A quick glance showed he was nearing the fence line and he thought he would be glad to get to the trees because they would at least provide some protection from the wind, and maybe the going would be a little easier. At least he hoped so.

THE FALLING LOGS IN THE STOVE STARTLED TAMMY AND she jumped in the rocker, dropping her book to the floor. She realized what had happened and laughed at herself, she was so immersed in the story the falling logs brought her back to reality. She looked at the Seth Thomas wind-up clock on the sideboard and saw it was getting close to 11:00. She scooted from the rocker and went to the front window, pushed aside the curtain, and wiped the frost from the pane with her warm hand and looked out, hoping to see Tommy returning. She squinted, rubbed the frosty window again and peered out into the white-out. The snowflakes were lazily drifting down so the wind had subsided, but the snow was so heavy she couldn't even see the barn. She dropped her eyes to the floor, thinking about her brother out there in the storm. Once again rubbing the window, hoping it was just the frost, but it was even worse, now the wind was picking up again. She started back to the rocker, voicing her thoughts out loud, "Oh Tommy! You better hurry up and get back here. If you don't get back 'fore Ma gets home, you're gonna be in so much trouble!" She reached down and picked up the Afghan and her book, stood tiptoe before the rocker and scooted back into the chair, opening the book to find her way back to her refuge.

TOMMY DUCKED INTO THE TREES, WATCHING WHERE the tracks of the deer led. He was envious of the deer, able to bounce through the snow and into the woods almost effortlessly. He wished he hadn't shot it, but his family needed the meat and he was determined to see his plan through. The snow was less than six inches deep in the pasture what with the wind whipping it about, but now in the trees, it was stacking up and it was well over the tops of his shoes and getting up in his trouser legs. He looked at the tracks of the fleeing deer, saw another drop of blood and looked up at the falling snow. He knew he was close to the deer, otherwise the blood would have been covered by the fresh snow. Encouraged, he pushed on, each step getting more and more difficult. He had to lift his foot high out of his own tracks and reach far forward for his next step. It was easier than dragging his feet through the deepening snow.

The rifle seemed to be getting heavier, he stumbled and fell face forward, trying to catch himself with the rifle. He pushed up out of the snow, struggled back to his feet and saw the snow all over the rifle. He brushed off the .22, thinking he had to have it ready in case he came upon the deer and had to shoot it again, but he fashioned a sling from the twine and slung it across his back.

It seemed like he had been fighting the snow for so long, he stopped and looked at the tracks. Now the snow was filling them in and it had been some time since he saw any blood, he didn't know if it was because the fresh snow covered it, or if the deer's wound was closing up and had quit bleeding. If so, that meant he wasn't badly wounded and might keep going and he would never catch up with it. He let out a heavy sigh, looking around at unfamiliar trees and spaces. He turned in his steps, looking back at his trail and saw the heavy snow was fast covering his tracks as well. He had never been this far into the woods and he wasn't sure where he was, what if he couldn't find his way back?

He had to decide, should he keep after the deer or start for home. He had lost track of the time but knew he had been following the deer tracks for quite some time and he had to be back at the house before his Ma got home or he would be in a lot of trouble, especially for leaving Tammy alone. The wind was picking up and whistled through the trees, now heavily laden with snow, their boughs drooping but the beauty was lost on Tommy. He felt the cold clawing at his neck and wrists, the icy air making his eyes water, and as his scarf drooped from his face, he pushed at it with a snow-covered mitten. He looked at the tracks of the fleeing deer, turned back to look at his own tracks where he slogged through the snow, then down at his feet and saw the snow was knee-deep. He knew it was going to be hard to push back through this snow to make it home, but the sooner he started the better.

He turned his back on the sign of the deer, looked to his back trail and saw his tracks were now no more than slight dips in the snow. He leaned forward, back to the wind, and took his first step homeward. Every step was a struggle and he was tiring fast, his heavy breathing and hot air began to form icicles on his scarf, and even his eyebrows. He was getting colder with each breath and every step, he could barely feel his feet, yet every step was hurting. Maybe if he could find some place out of the wind, stop and rest for a short spell and perhaps get warm.

He slogged on, unable to see his backtrail, the wind making it totally disappear and leaving no trace of his passing.

He remembered his Pa talking about how the wide branches of a pine, especially the spruce, would hold the snow and even make a bit of a shelter under those branches. He stopped and searched the nearby trees, each one seeming to whisper at him with the wind passing through the branches. There! That looked like what his Pa described, that big spruce. He pushed toward the towering tree, thinking if there were some pine needles and small branches, maybe he could start a fire and get warm. As he neared, he craned side to side, and it looked promising. He dropped to his hands and knees, with his rifle now slung over his back with the twine as a sling, he crawled under the humbled branches and found his shelter. He crawled up next to the trunk, took his rifle from his back and stood it beside the trunk, and leaned back. He drew his knees up to his chest and wrapped his arms around them, trying for a little warmth. He thought he would just sit for a spell, then maybe try to start a fire. He had his Pa's flint and steel and a little tinder in his pack which now sat at his side. He smiled at the thought and his tiredness seemed to sap all his strength and he dropped his chin to his knees, to rest a while.

TAMMY WAS STARTLED WHEN SHE HEARD FOOTSTEPS ON the porch and she dropped her book to her lap as she stared at the door. The wind whooshed into the room carrying a snowy and bundled Amy, with Rebekah and Pastor Davis right behind. They were laughing and wiping snow from their hats and arms as they stomped their feet free of snow.

Tammy sat spellbound with her mouth slightly open and eyes wide as the three shrugged off their coats.

Amy said, "I'll get the water on and have that tea ready in just a moment. You really need to warm up before you start back." She looked at her daughter in the rocking chair and said, "Well, look at you little princess, are you enjoying my rocking chair?"

"Ummhumm," said Tammy, obviously a little concerned about something.

Amy looked around, looked up at the loft and called, "Tommy, come on down, we have company!" When there was no reply or movement, she looked at Tammy, "Is he out in the barn?" Tammy shook her head and dropped her eyes. Amy thought her heart skipped a beat as she knelt in front of her daughter, "What is it? Where is he?"

With big tears welling up in her eyes, Tammy tried her best to explain to her Mother about Tommy's plan to help with the family's need for fresh meat. "And with Pa worried about the banker, he just wanted to help and so did I."

Amy jumped to her feet and went to the door, jerked it open and stepped to the porch. She looked in the direction of the pasture but couldn't even see the near corral. The big heavy snowflakes were like a wall of white cotton before her. She spun on her feet and stepped back through the door, looking first to Tammy and then to the Pastor and his wife. "Pastor, I hate to ask, but could you go back to town and to the mill to tell Tom? I'm afraid our boy will be lost in this storm and we've got to find him!" she pleaded desperately. She looked at Rebekah, "Could you stay with Tammy, I've got to go look for Tommy," her eyes were begging for help.

Both Pastor and Rebekah nodded and said, "Of course." Pastor Davis went to the rack for his coat, followed closely by Amy who reached for hers as well. When the Pastor stepped through the door, Amy turned to Rebekah, "I won't go far, I'm just going to check the barn and corrals, maybe a little into the pasture, but I won't be long. I've got to do something, he's my boy," her eyes were showing tears and her voice cracked as she explained. She draped the scarf over her head and tucked it into her coat, turned to smile at her daughter and opened the door. Rebekah went to the window and rubbed off the frost as she tried to see where Amy went, a tug at her sleeve told of Tammy nearby. The girl looked up at her Pastor's wife and asked, "Is Tommy going to be alright?"

She knelt to be eye to eye with the girl and with her hands on her shoulders, Rebekah said, "I'm sure he will be fine. He probably just got turned around in the storm and is waiting for someone to come show him the way home. But how about you and me praying for him, alright?"

Tammy nodded her head as Rebekah took her little hands in her own and bowed her head and closed her eyes as she began, "Dear Lord, we ask you now to put your arms around Tommy and keep him safe. Guide his Mom and Dad and help them to find him soon and bring him home. We ask this now in Jesus' name. Amen." As she lifted her eyes to Tammy's, she heard a tiny "Amen" from the innocent child and smiled at the simple faith of the little one.

THE PASTOR STARTED OFF IN HIS BUGGY, WHIPPING HIS horse into a canter and ducking his head to let his hat brim deflect the snow from his face. Within moments he was at the end of the roadway and turning onto the main road but pulled his horse to a stop when the wagon of Tom Turner almost collided with him in the storm. "Whoa up there, Tom!" yelled the Pastor to be heard over the whistling wind. He heard the deep voice of Tom call "Whoa!" as he leaned back on the reins of his team.

Tom leaned down to look at the Pastor who stared from under the canvas top of his buggy. He listened as the Pastor began, "Tom, your wife sent me to get you."

"Whatever for? Surely, she's not afraid of a little storm, and by the way, Pastor, thanks for bringing her home. Now what is it that she's so concerned about?" he chuckled, thinking his wife was sometimes easily upset and could even be described as an alarmist.

"It's your boy, Tommy. Seems he went out hunting and has not returned, she's afraid he's lost in the storm." Both men had to speak rather loudly, and it was difficult to see each other through the snow. When Tom did not immedi-ately respond, the Pastor asked, "Did you hear me Tom?"

"Yes, I heard. I was looking at this snow, I'm afraid that boy's got himself into quite a predicament. I best hurry!" He picked up the reins but was stopped by the Pastor.

"I'll go into town and see if I can get a few men to come and help. The boy needs to be found soon!"

"Thanks Pastor, that'll help, but hopefully I can find him before that's necessary." Without saying more, he slapped the horses with the reins and disappeared in the snow.

Pastor Davis watched him go, and quickly gigged his horse into a canter to get into town and get some help right away. As he thought about who could help and where he could find them, different names came to mind but being new, he still did not know where everyone lived. Maybe he could get some help at the grocery, it would still be open, and John McPherson would know who else might be able to help.

TOM PULLED UP IN FRONT OF THE BARN, JUMPED DOWN and slid the big door aside and led the horses and buggy into the big barn. He dropped the reins and slid the big door closed. Even though it was mid-day, the snow let little light through and he had to light a lantern. Just as he lowered the chimney, the back door opened and he turned, hoping to see Tommy coming through, but it was Amy. She didn't know Tom had returned and as she turned to shut the small door, she was startled when she heard his voice.

"What are you doing out in this storm?" he growled, but he knew she had undoubtedly been looking for Tommy. "I'm sorry," and held out his arms as she came near, "I just hoped you were Tommy coming in. I know you were looking for him, any sign?"

She shook her head and dropped her forehead to his shoulder, "It's so cold out there, oh Tom, we've got to find him!"

He drew her close and hugged her tight, "We will, we will," he consoled. He pushed her back so he could look in her eyes, "Now, you go back inside and put together a pack of food for me, and make sure there's a handful of lucifers in the bag. And get my flint and steel and tinder out of my possibles bag, or just get the bag. I'll put up the horses and saddle Meg, then I'll come in and get some extra clothes and blankets 'fore I start out."

She nodded her head and tried to force a smile, then stepped around him and started for the house. Tom quickly unharnessed the horses and put them in their stalls, then started gearing up the mule. He slid the big door back just enough to get the mule through, pushed it shut and tethered the mule by the porch steps. Two long strides took him into the house and he went through his check list in his mind, making sure he had everything he needed. Amy had packed some jerky, sandwiches, dry beans and pork belly into the saddle bags. He took down the .25-35 and laid it on the table next to the bags.

When he came out of the bedroom, he had on his wool uniform britches and shirt, his heaviest union suit, a heavy wool sweater that had been his father's, and his high-topped lace up boots. Amy slipped a wool scarf around his neck and stood before him as he shrugged into his heavy Mackinaw showing the shearling lining as he buttoned it up. The collar stood around his neck and his floppy felt hat drooped over his ears. He reached for the rifle but was stopped by his wife, "You better kiss me before you load up, mister!" she tried to scowl but her face split into a smile as she looked at this man, her husband and her hero.

He pulled her close and kissed her gently, and they held each other tightly as they whispered into each other's ears the simple words of love and promise. Speaking softly, he told of the Pastor's plan to get help, "And if he does, I'll try to leave sign for them to follow. I might even come back a ways to find any others that are willing to brave this storm." A tug at his sleeve told Tom that Tammy also wanted a hug from her father, some reassurance that he would make everything alright and Tommy would soon be home. He dropped to one knee and drew her near and gave her a long hug. When she pulled back she started, "Will you bring..."

"Yes, sweetheart, I'm going out to bring Tommy home. You keep your Mom here and the two of you can pray for me to find Tommy soon. Will you do that?"

"Ummmhummm," she said as she nodded her head.

Tom stood and with the saddlebags and bedroll in one hand and the scabbarded rifle in the other, he went to the door, turned back for a smile from his girls, and stepped into the storm. He quickly tied on the saddle bags and bedroll, hung the scabbard under the stirrup fender on the right side, butt forward, and dusted the snow from the seat of the saddle before he swung aboard the impatient mule. Although Meg had stood patiently, when Tom reined her around, she started out at a quick step, impatient to get on the move.

Tammy had said Tommy was going to hunt the willows by the Little River and Tom was there within a few moments. He called out, but the wind was too much and even if Tommy heard him, he wouldn't be able to hear a reply. He dropped to the ground, tucked the end of the reins in his belt and walked beside the brush, kicking at any large cluster as he called out for his son. He walked the length of the willows until he reached the bridge. After crossing over, he went downstream on the opposite side, searching for any sign of Tommy's crossing or hiding out or any sign of deer that might have caused Tommy to give chase.

After a short distance, maybe thirty yards, something caught Tom's eye and he pushed away the brush. The heavy snow had weighed down the willows that covered the trail of the wounded deer coming from the river. Tom saw two distinct deer prints and a splatter of blood. He turned to look across the pasture for any other sign, but the wind-blown snow painted an empty canvas with no sign of any living thing. He looked back across the river to see if he could tell where the deer entered, then turned to look behind him to the woods. The snow was too heavy, and he couldn't even see the fence line.

He mounted up and tried to line out the direction the deer probably went. Pointing Meg toward where he knew the fence would be, he thought he could make a straight line to the fence, go to the gate and come back and pick up his line and head to the woods. After making his way through the gate and coming back to his starting point, he took a rag from his possibles bag and tied it to the fence as a sign for anybody that followed, then pointed Meg to the trees. Maybe he could find some sign in the woods where the trees would protect the trail from the wind.

AMY AND REBEKAH BUSIED THEMSELVES AT THE counter, preparing a pot of beef stew. The meat was already simmering in the big cast iron pot on the stove, and the ladies were peeling potatoes and slicing carrots, the last of the stored vegetables from the cellar. A big enamel pot of coffee was perking, and the smell of pot roast and fresh coffee filled the house. Tammy had resumed her place in the rocker and was content with her book. The ladies worked in silence, each filled with thoughts and hopes for Tommy.

The sudden knock on the door made everyone jump, and the ladies laughed at one another and Amy called out, "Come in!"

The pastor led two others into the house and all three stomped their feet and after removing their hats, unbuttoned their coats and greeted the ladies. John McPherson, the owner of the grocery, and Donovan Armbruster, the owner of the Jackson hotel, stood behind the Pastor. He asked, "Is that coffee ready? We sure could use a cup, if that's alright?"

Amy wiped her hands on her apron and stepped to the stove. She grabbed a pot holder and picked up the big pot and stepped to the table where sat several tin cups. She nodded to the men, "Have a seat, you need something warm. And, thank you for coming!"

"Yes'm, that's what neighbors do, m'am," said Armbruster. He reached for the steaming cup and brought it to his lips, sipping carefully of the black brew.

"What direction did your husband go, m'am," asked McPherson, holding his cup close to his chin and enjoying the steam from the cup and the warmth on his hands. Both men still had their coats on, though undone, and appeared anxious to get on with the task at hand.

"He said he would follow the willows along the river, and if he found any sign going away, he would follow it, but he would leave sign for anyone that followed."

"Good, good. That's what I was hopin', cuz we don't

have much daylight left, it's little enough as it is, and unless this storm lets up, it's not gonna be easy finding any sign."

Amy looked at John McPherson, then to the other men who were nodding their heads in agreement and she dropped into the nearby chair. She reached to set the coffee pot on the stove and lowered her head in her hands, trembling. She lifted tear-filled eyes to the men, saying nothing, then slowly stood and walked back to the counter.

The men whispered among themselves and the Pastor nodded as McPherson and Armbruster stood and doing up their coats, started for the door. Amy saw them start to leave and she called out, "Thank you men, thank you." They lifted a hand to wave and left, pulling the door shut behind them. The Pastor said, "They will try to find any sign your husband left and will do as much as they can, but if they run out of light, they'll be back." He stood and went to stand beside his wife, "Amy, Tommy is a very smart and resourceful boy and I'm sure his father taught him a lot about the woods and such. And Tom is no stranger to the laws of survival and with God in control, I believe we'll soon see them home. Now, how 'bout we gather at the table and have a prayer." The women nodded and went to the table, seated themselves and as Tammy stood beside her mother, everyone joined hands and the Pastor led in a prayer asking God for guidance and protection and the safety of Tommy and the searchers. After his "Amen" he said, "Amy, I'm going to head back home, but Rebekah will stay here with you. You'll probably need help to feed those hungry men when they get back and she'll be here to help. If they come back with Tommy tonight, then I'll thank you to bring Rebekah into church with you in the morning. But, if I don't see you there, I'll get more folks to help in the search and we'll find him tomorrow, and hopefully the storm will let up and it will be a lot easier."

"Thank you, Pastor. I don't know what I would have done without your help, and yours too, Rebekah. I'm so thankful." She daubed at her eyes, now reddened with the tears, and looked back at Pastor Davis. He touched her shoulder and said, "Well, maybe we'll just see your whole family in church in the morning and we'll all thank the Lord together."

"I hope so, I really do. And thank you again," said Amy as she turned to Tammy and let the Pastor and Rebekah have a few moments alone before he left.

TWILIGHT WAS FADING WHEN THE STOMPING OF FEET on the porch startled the women as they sat silently at the table, picking at their food. Amy jumped from her seat to go to the door and with her heart pounding and her eyes wide with expectancy and hope, she opened the door to see two men, snow covering their hats and shoulders as they tried to kick the snow from their boots. Donovan Armbruster looked up to the hopeful face of Amy and shook his head as he dropped his eyes. "I'm sorry, m'am, we couldn't hardly see Tom's trail, what with the wind and the snow, and when it faded out in the trees, we knew we couldn't help anybody if we got lost too. If'n you can spare a cup o' coffee, we'll warm up a mite and head back to town. After a night's rest and come daylight, we'll be right back at it."

Amy dropped her head and stepped back, holding the door open for the men and motioned to the table. "We have more than coffee, I'm sure you're hungry. Take off your coats and have a seat. I'll get some plates for you." She moved to the counter, her weak knees almost giving out and catching herself on the counter edge, she stood for a moment before reaching into the cabinet. She dished up big helpings of the stew and vegetables and set the plates before the men, dropping into her own chair. Rebekah had poured the men some coffee and with heavy sighs, the men started working at their supper. Amy spoke softly, "I'm very thankful for you men going out in this terrible storm and all. I feel so helpless here at home," she waved her hand around to indicate the warm house, "and I'm so worried about Tommy and now Tom." Her voice faded as she dropped her head to her hands.

The men looked helplessly at the woman, wishing they could do more, but even words of comfort and hope were not forthcoming. They looked at one another, wolfed down their food and stood to excuse themselves. "M'am, thank you kindly for the meal and coffee. We'll be goin' now, but we'll be back at first light and we'll do our best to get your menfolk back," explained John McPherson as the men backed toward their coats and the door.

Amy looked up at them and added, "Again, thank you men. I do greatly appreciate it."

Rebekah stood and walked closer to the men, speaking softly, "If you go by the parsonage, please stop in and tell my husband," she dropped her head and lifted it again, "well, tell him of your efforts and plans. And I thank you as well."

"Yes'm, we will certainly stop and tell him. I wish we could do more, but when we can't see anything, what with the storm and now the dark, well, you understand, don't you ma'am?"

"Yes, of course. We know you've done all you can and thank you."

Typical of winter in the Rockies, the storm lost

its fervor just after midnight and dawn came with shades of pink and orange reflecting off the pristine white blanket. The morning revealed a clear blue sky and a silent beauty across the countryside. And true to the times, a fresh snowfall did little to deter the crowd that attended church on that beautiful morning. While most families came by horse drawn wagons or buggies, there were a few of the more well-to-do families that came in their automobiles. The usual collection of autos, wagons, and buggies were to be seen beside the corrals that held the various teams of horses that were tromping down the snow before the lean-to sheds. Well bundled families climbed the few steps and entered the warm sanctuary of Community Church, each welcomed by the pastor.

Although the word had passed among several of the families about the lost child of the Turner family, not everyone knew. There was a more somber mood than usual that settled over the crowd, but many were seen greeting one another and shaking hands before finding their seats. And although the usual routine would see the service start with some hymn singing, their regular pianist was not present as the pastor walked to the pulpit.

"Good morning, everyone," he greeted as he held his hands up for their attention. "It's good to see everyone out on this beautiful morning, even with all the snow." He smiled and nodded his head as several chuckles were heard. "This morning, I'm going to do something a little different than what you're used to, or what you might expect. You see, it's easy for us to fall into the routine of our church service, we gather together, sing some songs, have a prayer, and then patiently listen to whatever the pastor has prepared in the days leading up to Sunday. But I believe that what the pastor preaches is not to be something that impresses you the congregation about how much the pastor has learned, but rather something that you can apply to your life.

"The Bible teaches that to be a Christian is to be Christlike, or to learn to do what Christ would do in whatever situation we find ourselves. Now, last week I spoke about how we are to love one another, as Christ loves us and as we love ourselves." Several of the crowd nodded their heads and many added an "Amen."

"So, keeping that in mind, I had to ask myself, If Jesus were here, would He want us to listen to another, maybe boring, sermon. Or would he want us to apply what we have learned, or literally, do what the Bible say to do. And of course, my answer was the doing of it. So, this morning, we have an opportunity to do," he paused when he saw one of the more elderly ladies raise her hand with a bit of a scowl on her face. "Yes, Mrs. Dinwoody?"

"Pastor, are you saying we're not going to have a sermon today? I can't believe you would do that, I mean, after all, we came out to have church and hear a sermon!"

"Mrs. Dinwoody, I appreciate you wanting to hear a sermon, but if all we do is listen to sermons and never apply what we hear, what good is a sermon?" Again, there were several that sounded an "Amen" from the crowd. He lifted his eyes to the crowd and said, "Perhaps some of you have not heard, but little Tommy Turner, a boy of nine, going on ten, years old, felt compelled to help his family, that's going through some hard times, by going hunting for some venison. But, he got caught in the storm and is now lost in the mountains. His father has gone searching, and a couple of our men, Mr. Armbruster and Mr. McPherson, are also out searching. I believe we as a church must 'get with the doing of it' and put our works with our words." Many enthusiastic "Amens" were heard as he paused. "So, I suggest we get with

Sheriff Showalter and put together as big a search party as possible and find little Tommy. Now ladies, we don't expect you to mount a horse and go into the woods, not that you couldn't and many of you could do just as good a job as most men, but we will need you to prepare some food. The Turner's cellar is pretty empty, so if you ladies could go home and prepare a dish of food, preferably something hot, and bring it to the Turner home, that will help the many searchers that will gather there. And those of you men that are willing to help in any way, Sheriff Showalter will be here at the front to get things organized. Now, let's all join hands for prayer."

The pastor stepped from behind the pulpit and joined hands with those on the front row and began to pray. "Our Father in Heaven, oh how we need you today. Little Tommy Turner is somewhere out in those mountains, probably very afraid and very cold and he needs to be found..." He continued for a few moments asking for direction and protection for all the searchers as well as Tom and Tommy Turner, comfort for the family, and strength for Tommy. When he finished, his Amen was echoed by everyone present and the crowd moved, some of the ladies to organize their food preparation and the men to join with the Sheriff.

Less than an hour later, there was a veritable parade of wagons, buggies and horses moving up the road towards the Turner place. Some of the wagons, with baskets and boxes loaded, had horses tied on behind as did some of the buggies. Only one automobile had joined the crowd, the runabout of the Armbruster's and driven by Minerva Armbruster. Conspicuously absent was the grand Stephens Touring Car owned by J.B. Randall, the president of the bank and the chairman of the deacon board at the church. No one had expected the portly president to mount a horse and join the search, for none believed the man could even mount a horse, but he and his wife could have joined the efforts by bringing some food or helping in other ways. But as is often the case with those whose dignity and standing are as much pretense as anything, none were surprised at his absence.

Sheriff Showalter and his deputy, Gerald Whitcomb, were waiting at the Turner's as everyone arrived. The deputy stood at the corral gate, directing everyone to put their horses into the corrals, while the Sheriff motioned for the men to join him in the barn. He had placed a couple of boards over the sawhorses and had lain out a map of the area.

Amy and Rebekah were somewhat overwhelmed at the number of people that arrived and as the ladies filed up the porch steps, arms full of dishes and baskets, they welcomed each one and Amy directed the bearers of dishes to place them on the counter and the table. Several ladies had also brought more table ware, tin plates, cups, other items which were quickly laid in orderly fashion on both the sideboard and the counter.

The Sheriff was an old hand at organizing searches and readily applied his expertise in assigning groups of men together with a designated leader and a secondary leader. Each group had five men on horses or mules and were given a specific area to search. There were two that did not have horses and the Sheriff assigned them the task of taking a couple of wagons back to town to get some hay and grain for all the searcher's animals. Once everyone knew their assignments, the Sheriff suggested, "Be sure to get some food to take with, I'm sure you'll get hungry out there. The ladies will put together some for you, just take your saddle bags or what-have-you into the house and they'll fix you up."

Armbruster and McPherson had explained to Amy where they last saw sign of Tom and said they would start at that point and begin their search. When she relayed this information to the Sheriff, he adjusted his search plans accordingly and had directed each team of searchers correspondingly. By mid-morning, three teams were seen crossing the pasture and making for the bridge to find their way into the woods and start the search. Hopes were high, and everyone was optimistic.

Even the ladies in the house were planning the meals with positive thoughts and hopes. Once the ladies finished their preparations and had the oven and stove overloaded with food, Rebekah called them all together for a time of prayer. Each lady stole glances at Amy, feeling her fear and pain and wondering how they would respond if it were their child out there. Amy was comforted by the compassion of her friends and neighbors, but she still struggled to keep her thoughts positive and hopeful.

He heard them before he saw them. He guessed it to be two men by the noise they were making, not only the sounds of their horses grunting and forcing their way through the snow, but the broken branches they pushed aside and broke as well. But the giveaway had been their repeated calling at the top of their lungs for Tommy. He had started to mount Meg when he first heard them and now decided to wait for them to join in his search. He had spent a restless and cold night under his hastily made lean-to beside the deadfall pine. The downed tree had provided a bit of a windbreak for both him and his mule, but he added to it with several pine branches woven together as shelter from the continuing snow storm. It was difficult to keep a fire going, but with a slab of stone as a reflector and ample firewood with the branches of the snag, he did get a little sleep.

"Yo!" he called as the men drew near.

They answered with a loud, "Tom? Is that you?"

He lifted his voice, "It better be me, otherwise it's the ghost of Christmas past!"

He had his fire rekindled and blazing by the time they dismounted. They stepped to the fire and held out cold hands to gather in some of the heat. Armbruster asked, "Any sign of the boy?" It was a question that had to be asked, but he knew if Tom had found sign, he would be hot on the trail and not waiting to visit with them.

Tom shook his head, "None, not a one. That snow was just too much and covered up everything. When I started, I saw where he shot a deer and started after it, but the snow was so thick the tracks were covered. All I could do was go in the direction the deer started, but there was nothing. The wind was so loud it didn't help to call out. Even if he heard me, I wouldn't have heard him answer." He explained, dropping his head as he shook it side to side.

McPherson spoke up, "When we started after you yesterday, we found the rag you tied to the fence, and started into the trees, but like you said, the wind and the snow, well..."

Armbruster said, "I think the pastor's gonna get the sheriff to put together a search party today, at least that's what he said last night. But we didn't want to wait, that's why we're here now. What do you suggest?"

Tom stretched his hands to the flames, and said, "Before you showed up, I was gonna start circlin' or movin' back an' forth across the hillside here abouts. There's plenty of trees and gullies an' such, he might have found cover. I taught him about usin' the branches of a tree, you know, how the branches bend under the snow and make a kind of hole by the trunk. He might've found cover under a big tree, an' there's some overhangs and caves an' such around these hills, but they'll be hard to find with all the snow."

"So, if we spread out a little and work our way across

these ridges, you think we might find some sign?" asked Donovan.

"I hope so, but if he's not up and movin', there won't be much sign. But mebbe if he's holed up under a tree or sumpin', mebbe he'll hear us callin' and respond. So, I reckon we'll have to stop and go, call out and see what we find." He kicked snow on the fire as did the other men and they mounted up to start their search.

THE SNOW WAS DEEP BUT THE WARM SUN AND THE balmy temperature of 40^0 had already started the snow settling and the limbs of the pines and spruce were letting slip their scarves of white and springing back to show more green than white. The three searchers had spread out to work their way up the wide draw and timbered hillside. They had chosen to continue on a straight-line search from the last point. The slope of the hill faced the northeast, or the coldest side of any mountain in the Rockies, and the snow did little settling among the trees. As Tom nudged Meg forward, he approached a tall big trunked spruce with long limbs that hung to the snow. There was something about the snow, what appeared to be a trail or tracks that showed as nothing more than a slight dip in the smooth snow, but he moved closer and stepped down for a closer look. What he saw appeared to be a trail that led under the big branches, but also just a few feet beyond appeared to lead away.

He waded through the deep snow and bent low to try to see through the branches and the small space between the limbs showed something that roused his curiosity. He slapped at the snow on the branches, knocking them free and had to lean back away as the limb, relieved of its burden, sprung up to its original position. Tom ducked under and crawled on all fours into the shadowy hollow. He lifted his eyes to look around and froze, unable to even breathe, as he saw the .22 rifle leaning against the trunk of the tree. He swung around for any other sign of his boy, and seeing nothing, he grabbed for the rifle and pulled it against his chest, breathing deeply. *He was here! We're on the right trail!* He scurried back out and lifted his voice to call the others. "John! Donovan! Over here!"

Within moments the two men joined Tom by the big spruce, both immediately dropping to the ground to see the rifle. "This is Tommy's! He was here!" he pointed to the grotto under the branches, "In there! We're on the right track!"

John McPherson bent down and crawled under the branches to see where the boy had been, looking carefully for any other sign, something to give them hope. On the far edge, where the branches did not hang as low, he looked and saw a track, and another. He shook his head and looked at the branches and plucked a tuft of fur from one. He backed out and stood up beside the other men and with a somber face he turned to the boy's father. Tom saw his expression and asked, "What is it? What'd you see?"

John held out the tuft of brown fur and said, "And there's a couple of tracks there, on the far side. And Tom, there's more."

It was a frightened face that looked to John, waiting for more.

"There's drag marks. It looks like," and he took a step around the low hanging branches, "he came out this way," he turned and searched the trees and the hillside, "maybe went thataway," pointing between two ponderosa that stood on the steep slope.

"No! No! It can't be!" declared Tom as he dropped to all fours and crawled back into the branch lined hollow. He went to where John saw the tracks and there in the drifted snow, two tracks, unmistakably grizzly tracks, and what could only be drag marks. The snow from the branches and wind marred the edge of the third track as they disappeared under the branches and into the snow beyond. Tom dropped his tear-filled eyes to the ground and fell back on his side, wanting to curl up and die thinking of his boy, little Tommy, in the clutches of a grizzly.

With a deep breath and renewed resolve, he crawled back out and stood beside the now silent men. John looked at his friend, "Tom, we don't know what happened. Maybe Tommy was gone by the time the bear came, and that could have been anything he was dragging out. Maybe even part of a deer that Tommy shot." Tom just looked at his friend and then dropped his head, kicking at the snow at his feet.

"It could be that Tommy skedaddled well before the bear came and we'll find him hiding out in another tree hanging just like this!" encouraged Donovan.

John spoke up, "Tom, I'm pretty sure the pastor and sheriff have some others out searching by now. Maybe we should try to join up with them and we can concentrate our search from this point. With all of us focused on this area, we're bound to find him soon!" It was as much of a question as a comment, but both men knew what he was implying, that they would find Tommy's body soon, after the bear had finished with it.

Tom took a deep breath, shrugged his shoulders and said, "Sure, I'll stay here and start a fire, so we can start from here. You two go back and find the searchers and bring them up." Both men looked at Tom and John asked, "Are you going to be alright?"

"No. No, I won't be alright until my son is alright. But I'll be here waiting. Now, go on and get the others."

"TOMMY WAS WEARING A BROWN COAT WITH DARK brown fur collar and lining. His cap was dark brown, almost black and we think he had on his dark green corduroys. He also had mittens and high-top lace up shoes." Tom was speaking to the men of the three search teams. Armbruster and McPherson had returned with them and counting Tom, there were now eighteen men ready to search. "John, you take the end of the line on the uphill side, and Donovan, if you'll take the end down in the draw, then the rest of us will space out within sight of each other and move across the face of this slope together. I'm sure I don't need to tell you, but with what we found, we need to look for anything that might be Tommy's and also look for any place that might be a likely spot for a hibernating bear. I know, bears are supposed to be hibernating all winter, but the oldtimers will tell you it's not unusual for a grizzly to crawl out and go looking for food and then go back to his hidey-hole. So, keep your eyes peeled, and your rifles ready, because if this'ns still huntin' food, we don't want any of us to be his supper." The listeners shook their heads, mumbled their agreement, and kicked at the snow. They knew how hard it was for Tom to even think about his son being with the bear, but until they knew otherwise, there was always hope.

Tom looked at the sun, calculated it to be just past mid-day, and mounted up to take his place in the line. Rather than fill a particular spot, he planned to move about on the sure-footed Meg and cover ground that others might find too challenging. He wanted to be certain that every square foot of this mountain was searched and searched thoroughly.

IT WAS A LONG LINE OF MEN THAT RODE BACK TO THE house, heads hanging and tired horses dragging feet in the wet snow. The sun had already dropped beyond the western mountains and the colors of days end had faded from the sky. Dusk was dropping its curtain on the long day and the men and horses were tired and disappointed. After struggling through the snow on the steep mountainside, the searchers had pushed to the top of the ridge and the end of the narrow valley, turned and did the same on the opposite side. Hope had soared early in the afternoon when one mitten that was identified as Tommy's was found by Franklin Forrester, the blacksmith, and Tom was excited to see there were no teeth or claw marks on the mitten, no evidence it had been touched by a bear. He thought maybe, just maybe, Tommy had escaped the hollow under the tree before the bear came. But with no other sign of any kind, hopes slowly faded and the men had to return to the house.

When the women saw them coming in, they scurried around setting the food out and making everything ready for the tired and undoubtedly hungry men. There was no question their search had been fruitless, the slow movements, hanging heads, somber expressions told the story. But questions had to be asked and answered. The men had agreed to keep mum about the bear, knowing the added worry would accomplish nothing, especially for the mother of the boy. At any other time, a gathering of this size around a meal, talk would flow as freely as the coffee was poured, but only whispered exchanges, or softly voiced questions and answers were to be heard.

Amy and Tom had retreated to their bedroom with only Tammy and the pastor and his wife joining them. The sobbing of the mother and low uttered words of hope and encouragement could be heard through the door and many of the women and a few of the men allowed tears to fall in sympathy. Slowly, the crowd left, most offering prayers and hope, but little could really be said when darkness mirrored the mood of the friends and neighbors.

The house had been tidied up and the remaining food was covered and placed on the counter. One of the men had put a large wooden box outside, laid it on its side, covered it with a tarp and heaped snow over the top. The women stacked dishes and pots of food inside and the lid was tacked up and snow stacked in front. They had agreed, if the search was to continue, the food would be needed, and if not, the family could use the help.

Amy and Tom talked well into the night, praying often and trying to think of any possible way the boy could still be alive and found. "I'm not going to give up! If I have to ride those mountains all day long every day, I'm going to find our boy. Just the thought of him out there by himself, wondering where his Daddy is, well..." he dropped his head and a heavy sob escaped and his shoulders shook as he tried to stifle another.

Amy reached her hand around his shoulder, "And I wouldn't ask you to stop. I can't help but think the same thing, our boy, so little, so helpless." She lay her head on his shoulder and cried. "Would it help if I came with you?" she pleaded, desperate to do anything she could to hasten her son's return.

"No, babe, you need to stay here and take care of our daughter. We can't forget her, she's scared and worried, just like we are, and she needs her mother beside her, don't you think?"

She lifted her embroidered hanky to her eyes and nodded her head, "Yes, you're right. Do you think she should go to school?"

"I dunno, it might help her being with other kids, and maybe not, they'd probably be asking her a bunch of questions she couldn't answer. And, I really don't want her walking to school by herself, it's just too cold out there and all, nah, keep her home with you."

Amy nodded her head, agreeing with her husband. She looked around their bedroom and added, "Just a couple of days ago, we were worried about losing this," motioning with a wave of her hand to indicate their home, "and I never thought there could be anything worse than losing your home, and now..." she dropped her head again and sobbed.

Tom put his arm around her shoulder and drew her near. "We haven't lost him yet! He could be sittin' out there under some big ol' tree, just waitin' to be found, and I'm gonna do it!" He stomped his foot to the floor in frustration to emphasize his resolve.

Amy held the found mitten on her lap and fingered it, thinking, and said, "I hope so, Tom, oh how I hope so."

. . .

Tom rode Meg across the meadow, its patches of snow glowing in the last of the moonlight, toward the bridge that would take him into the upper pasture. He looked at the field that had been cleared, groomed, and tended by both his father and him, thinking how this flat piece of land had been his father's hope for a better life for his family. *Yessir, son, with this field cleared and planted in grass, why, we can get us a herd o' cattle and before you know it, we'll be livin' high off the hog!* And now his father's dreams would be taken away by the greedy banker, J.B. Randall. And he would probably do with it like he did with the Smith place, just let the buildings fall in, the grounds around the house get overgrown, and use the pastures for his own cattle. Tom thought the banker was envious of the Hutchinson's, one of the first families to settle in the valley and to build a sizable ranch. But they had done it with hard work and sacrifice, not by ripping it out from under their neighbors.

As he thought about J.B., he remembered the kindly man and leader in the church. Before he was a deacon, he taught Sunday School and helped the pastor at every opportunity. He was known to have helped many families with groceries, a helping hand, and more. But John McPherson said that when J.B. got word of his son's death in the battle of the Argonne Forest in France, he became bitter and seemed to take it out on everyone around him. Tom also thought he was especially resentful with him since he had survived that same conflict and returned home. But he had not even known J.B.'s son, Jacob Jr., was in the army, much less in the same division. But 117,000 Americans and allies were killed or wounded in that battle and there was no way Tom could have known about Jacob. But now, he was beginning to know what J.B. felt at the loss of a son, he just prayed that loss would not be real and that he would find Tommy soon.

In the shadow of Cleveland mountain and its long spine that stretched south with the Poncha Pass road and Poncha creek skirting its eastern flank, was a smaller bald top ridge that lay to the east of the area searched by the men the previous day. Tom decided to ride the ridge top and search, then drop onto the east slope on his return to closely examine the hillside covered mostly by rock and juniper, for any possibility of a grizzly's lair or other sign of his son.

The wind and warm sunshine had mostly cleared the ridge of any remaining snow, but the occasional ravine still held the drifts and pockets of white. Climbing to the top of the ridge, Meg had to push through drifts that had packed heavy due to the warmer weather on Sunday. It was hard going, but when they topped out, Tom stepped down to put his binoculars to use and give the mule a bit of rest.

He seated himself on a warm slab of granite, drew his knees up to support his elbows and began his scan. Where he could see through the trees, he looked for any trails made by deer or elk or any other animal, grizzly included. But every patch of white lay unmarked and unbroken. He searched for any cave openings, and rocky outcropping that could hide an overhang or cutback that could be used for hibernating creatures. But from his vantage point, he saw nothing to buoy his hopes. He dropped his hand with the binoculars and looked around in the nearby trees and rocks, lifting his eyes to the sky that was empty of clouds and spread its arch of blue over the mottled landscape.

He sucked in a deep breath, stood and turned back to

mount Meg. He would ride the ridge to the south, drop into the narrow valley cut by some no-name creek that only held water in the spring and after a heavy rain but had a few cottonwood and aspen that marked the bottom. He would search the eastern slope of the ridge, any ravines that came from the top, and if there was time he would cross over to the west slope of the foothill ridges that came from Cleveland mountain. He gigged Meg and she started her long stride walk that would take them quickly down into the valley.

Tom had been gone from the house since about an hour before sunup and Amy was just tidying up her kitchen area when a knock on the door startled her. She caught her breath, and walked to the door, opening it to find John McPherson standing, hat in hand, and two other men behind him.

"Mornin' Amy, Tom around?"

"Morning John," and leaning to look to the other men, Donovan Armbruster and Franklin Forrester, the blacksmith, "gentlemen." She looked back at John, "No, Tom left early. Would you men like some coffee? I have a pot on."

John turned to look at the others who stood expressionless and back to Amy, "Well, since you've got it on, sure. But we won't take long, we want to get to the mountains."

Amy turned to the kitchen, leaving the door open for the men who stepped in and undid their coats, stomped their feet from any snow and mud, and walked to the table to have a seat. Amy set cups on the table, poured the steaming coffee and put the pot back on the stove. She sat at the table with the men and said, "I want to thank you men for what you're doing, it means so much to us."

"Well, it's the least we can do. We're neighbors and what happens to one of us, happens to all of us. But, enough of that, did Tom say where he was going to go today?"

"Yes, he did, and he told me that if anyone showed up to tell them all about it. He said he was going to the top of the bald ridge, you know the one above the washout, where that alluvial fan spreads out into the valley?" She looked around the table and only Donovan was nodding his head in understanding.

He looked at the others and said, "You know, that big washout that keeps gettin' bigger every time we have a big rain when the floodwaters come down those two ravines and bring all the gravel and mud with 'em."

"Oh yeah, I know where you're talkin' about. I just never heard it called that, whatever it was you said," replied John as he looked back to Amy.

She smiled and said, "Alluvial fan, where the water brings the gravel and silt, and it spreads out like a fan," she paused to see the other men nodding and grinning as they grasped what she explained. "Anyway, he's going up on that ridge, then down to the valley to the south and come back along the east slope of that ridge. If no one joins him, then he'll start back up the west slope across from the ridge."

All three men nodded, sipping their coffee, and when she paused, John replied, "Well, let's finish this," holding up his cup, "and get a move on. By the time we get there, we can start up the west slope and probably see Tom somewhere along in there. That way we'll cover more ground and increase our chances."

Amy caught the word, chances, and dropped her head knowing their efforts were just that, taking all the chances and checking every possibility. But that's what had to be done, the life of a youngster was at stake and even if the bear was not a part of his disappearance, the boy could not long survive alone in the woods in the winter. This was a hard country for men and women, harder still for youngsters.

Amy stood on the porch watching as the men rode across the meadow and on into the far pasture. With her arms crossed before her and the knitted wool stole over her shoulders, she said a silent prayer for the men, her husband, and her son. Hope rode with the men and she prayed this would not be another disappointing day.

WHEN SHE SAW FOUR MEN COMING ACROSS THE meadow, heads down, she knew they were unsuccessful in their search. As she strained to make out the shadowy figures in the dim light of dusk, she felt the burden of disappointment weighing upon her shoulders and pushing on her chest. It was a struggle to even breathe, and she leaned her forehead against the frosty window pane and felt lost, empty, drained. She took a deep breath, lifted her head and looked back at the divan and the tiny figure of Tammy, stretched out, her head on the small pillow, and innocence painted on her napping face.

Amy had done her best to keep her spirits up and share precious moments with her daughter, reading part of her borrowed book aloud and talking about the adventures of the girls in the story. In her innocence, Tammy asked, "Mommy, the girls in the story were lost in the woods too, and they came home. Can't Tommy come home too?"

"Yes, Tammy. Tommy could come home, but we have to find him first and that's what your daddy and the other men are doing, searching for Tommy."

"I want Tommy home and he has to be here for the Christmas program. He's the Innkeeper!"

"I want him home too, Tammy. And we need to pray that the Lord will bring him home in time for the program. We can do that can't we?"

"Ummhummm," answered the child, her eyes heavy. Amy fluffed up the small pillow and helped Tammy stretch out on the divan and kissed her closed eyes as she drifted off to sleep.

Amy walked to the stove, moved the big coffee pot to the front and the hotter burner, opened the oven door and struggled with the heavy cast-iron lidded pot and set it on top of the stove. She lifted the lid, potholder in hand, and used the long handled wooden spoon to stir the chicken and gravy in the bottom, trying not to disturb the dumplings resting on top. She replaced the lid, tiptoed to lift the rolling front of the warming oven and checked on the peach cobbler, or spider cake, in the cast iron skillet staying warm. Satisfied that all was ready, she walked back to the window to await the men. When she heard footsteps on the porch, she rose and opened the door to admit Tom, John, Donovan, and Franklin.

Their tiredness was evident by their shuffling steps, their disappointment was painted on their faces and Amy stood silently. Tom put his arms around her waist and bent to kiss her, but she turned her head and put her forehead on his chest as she grabbed handfuls of his Mackinaw and gritted her teeth, slightly banging her head on Tom's chest but not saying a word. Tom pulled her tight to him and bent his head beside hers and held her.

The men were uncomfortable at the emotion, but Tom motioned with his hands and they understood, removed their coats and hats and went to the table. Within moments,

Amy pulled back from Tom, wiped her face with her apron, and went to the stove to get the coffee. With the end of her apron, she picked up the coffee pot, and with a potholder in the other hand, she held the lid as she poured the coffee into the tin cups for the men. She retrieved the big pot of chicken and dumplings, set it in the middle of the table, and lay the ladle beside it. She nodded to Tom, and he reached to remove the lid and started filling the tin plates for the men. Amy left the table and went into her bedroom, closing the door behind her, and sat in her rocker, staring at the frosted window.

Tom saw the handle of the skillet sticking out of the warming oven and when he opened it up, he was pleased to see his favorite spider cake, peach cobbler. He spooned out big helpings for each of the men, Franklin saying, "Well, I didn't think I'd be able to come out again in the mornin', but I think I'd even walk all over them mountains for another helpin' of this!" The others chuckled and agreed, and John said, "Well, I don't think I can make it tomorrow. What with the holidays, we're pretty busy at the store and Milly's gonna need my help. But if you're still at it later in the week, I'll sure come back, Tom."

"Well, I can come tomorrow, but not the next day, if that'll be a help Tom," added Donovan. "That'll make three of us, countin' you of course."

"That'll be fine, Donovan. I'll wait for you fellas before headin' out tomorrow. But I do want to get as early a start as possible. I think we'll work that west slope above Little Cochetopa creek tomorrow. I really don't think he coulda got that far, but ya just never know." The men, busy at their desert, nodded their heads in agreement.

. . .

AFTER THE MEN LEFT, TOM TURNED TO HIS SLEEPING daughter, picked her up and carried her into her bedroom and lay her on her bed. The girl stirred but felt the familiar pillow case and pulled the pillow closer. Tom removed her shoes and socks, helped her into her nighty, and kissed her goodnight as she snuggled down into her bed and underneath her favorite quilt. Tom tiptoed from the room and went to the stove to stoke it up for the night, adjusted the dampers and turned back to the table. He sat the pot with the chicken and dumplings in the warming oven beside the almost empty skillet with the spider cake. He scraped the plates, emptied the dregs from the coffee cups, scooted the coffee pot off the burner, and looked around. Satisfied, he started for the bedroom. He knew he had been stalling, fearful of facing his disappointed wife, but feeling every bit of her pain and disappointment. He pushed the door open, looked into the dark room and saw his wife, sitting in the rocking chair, moonlight streaming through the window and illumining her face. She looked at Tom and back to the window, unmoving.

He knelt down beside her rocker, took her hand in his, "I'm sorry babe, not a sign. But, I'm not giving up, I feel it in my heart that our boy is still out there, still waitin' to be found. I wish I could tell you when or where, but I can't. All I know is, I'll keep at it, no matter what."

Amy looked down at him, her lips pinched tightly together, and back to the window. She dropped her head and softly said, "I know you're doing everything you can, it's not your fault, I know that. But I'm scared, so scared and afraid for Tommy, and, and, . . . I'm mad! I can't help it, I'm mad! Why? Why? Why? I don't understand it! I've been arguing with God all day! I've prayed and asked, begged, pleaded, promised, did everything I know and nothing! It's like Heaven is made of brass! Everything just gets thrown back in my face with no answer!" She dropped her head in her hands and began to sob, tears wet her hands and dripped to her nightgown. She beat her hands on her knees, sobbing uncontrollably, and muttering, "Why? Why? Why?"

Tom pulled her close to him, burying her face in his chest and held her tight, letting her beat against his chest, and cry herself out. Tears flowed from his eyes unhindered, and he sniffled, and wiped tears and sniffles from his face. He wanted to scream and cry too, but Amy needed him to be strong and he stayed silent, holding her, waiting.

As TOM READIED HIS GEAR, HE GATHERED UP HIS CAMP coffee pot, some coffee and four cups. He had packed a parfleche with extra blankets, food, and the coffee pot and would tie it behind his saddle. Amy and Tammy were still abed, and he moved quietly out into the dim light of early morning. He wanted to be ready to go when the others arrived and dropped his gear on the porch, went to the barn and saddled up Meg. Typical of the mule, she wasn't cooperative this early in the morning, but she soon yielded, and he led her from the barn. He had just finished tying his gear on when he saw the men coming down the roadway. He had expected just Donovan and Franklin, but there were three. As they neared, he recognized the lean figure of Joe Hutchinson, he was the second generation of the earliest settlers in the area and had weathered much of the early years beside his father as they built their ranch, the largest in the valley.

"Howdy men," said Tom as he swung aboard the mule. He looked to Joe and said, "Thanks for coming Joe, and you too, Donovan and Franklin. I appreciate it. Did these two tell you what the plan was for today?"

"That's one o' the reasons I came, Tom. Figgered you needed another hand, and even with four of us, that West slope above the Cochetopa will take some searchin'. There's lots o' ridges and ravines on that side."

"You're right about that. Maybe if we just take the upper half on the way up and the lower half on the way back, we'll get 'er covered, ya' think?"

The seasoned rancher nodded his head in agreement and the men started out. As they crossed the pasture meadow, Joe looked at Tom's cattle and commented, "Your cattle are lookin' good Tom. How many?"

"Only 'bout thirty cows, but they're all bred. Lost one a while back to a cougar."

"Heard 'bout that. He got his licks in on you 'fore you done him in is what I heard. You doin' alright now?"

"Yeah, I forgot all about it what with the searchin' an' all. But I been keepin' my eyes open. Sometimes them mountain lions travel in pairs an' I don't cotton to another set to. Don't know if the men told you, but we saw grizzly tracks where we found the boy's rifle, and some drag marks, so the boy mighta been taken."

"Well, let's hope not," answered Joe as he lifted his hat and ran his fingers through the graying hair.

THE MORNING SUN WAS AT THEIR BACK WHEN IT painted the eastern sky with its colors of pink and orange, casting a glow across the mountains and making the patches of snow, still held among the trees, look like dollops of his wife's strawberry pudding. He let a grin cross his face as he thought of it and looked up to see they had come to the point of the foothills that told of the Little Cochetopa creek.

"Hey, lookee there, Tom. That's one o' them, whatcha-callits that your woman told about. One o' them fan things." Franklin was pointing to the washout that was the result of many spring floods and summer thunderstorms that washed the gravel and silt from the top of the mountain and down the ravine that was cut by that same water.

"Oh, you mean an alluvial fan?" he asked, grinning at Franklin. The blacksmith was a big man, as were most smithys of the time, had to be to handle the heavy wagons, wheels, and farm equipment. And although a master craftsman with metal and wood, he had not had the opportunity to get much formal education but was always eager to learn and took pride in any new lesson learned.

"Yeah, that's it. Alluvial fan, interesting," he answered, grinning.

They spaced themselves out up along the hillside as agreed, and with Tom at the top of the ridge, they started through the scattered juniper and piñon and occasional spruce. The farther up the wide canyon they traveled, the timber changed with more ponderosa, spruce and fir. Men of the mountains could usually tell about what altitude they were by the different vegetation. As the woods showed more of the taller pine and spruce, they were nearing eight and nine thousand feet.

The going proved more difficult than the previous days. The western slope didn't get much sun until well after mid-day and the thicker timber shielded the snow, making the search tough. With several deep ravines near the top, many times the men had to dismount and lead their animals through the deep channels, and up the opposite side. To make it even more challenging, there had been some blowdowns in previous years and the woods were littered with down timber that was impossible to cross and sometimes obscured under deep snow. When they finally reached the end of this ridge, where it nosed into the west flank of Cleveland mountain, everyone, animals included, were ready for a rest. Tom led them to a broad flat shoulder that had been blown clear of snow and now bid both traveler and afternoon sun a welcome. There was some bunch grass for the animals and Tom started a small fire to put on the coffee pot. After melting several hands full of snow, they finally had enough water to start the coffee and while they waited, they made short work of Amy's left-over biscuits and meat.

The return search of the lower flanks of the mountain was just as difficult. There were fewer deep ravines, but the slope was steeper and no existing trail to follow. Several times the men had to lead their horses along the steep hillside, the frozen ground offering little in the way of footholds. Tom and his sure-footed mule had become quite adept at the difficult and rocky talus as they were farther up and crossed the challenging terrain, but Tom wanted to be nearer the rocky outcroppings to search for any caves or other areas that might appeal to a hibernating bear. But once again, the searchers were unsuccessful and when they came to the end of the hill, they broke into the open flats and started back to the house. It was late afternoon, and no more than an hour of daylight remained, and the men and animals were tired. But disappointment weighed heavy upon them and little was said as they neared the house.

Joe spoke for the others, "Tom, we're goin' to go on home. There's still enough light to get some chores done so you tell your wife goodbye for us, alright?"

"Sure Joe, and thanks for coming today, and likewise for

you two as well," he said as he nodded to Franklin and Donovan. "I appreciate all of you, more than I can say."

The men waved as they started down the roadway and Tom turned to the barn. He put Meg in her stall, hung the saddle on the fence and set the parfleche, saddle bags, and bedroll aside while he forked hay to the animals. He took a close look at Bossy, the milk cow, and could tell she had been milked and would be fine until time for her morning milking. He thought of Amy out here on the three-legged stool and milking the cow, and chuckled. It was probably her least favorite thing to do, but she had done it, and he was mighty proud of his wife. He picked up his gear and walked to the house with it's golden light in the window biding him welcome home.

Meg wasn't happy when Tom opened the stall to bring her out into the open area of the barn. She kicked out and almost caught him on the knee, but the narrow miss landed a solid blow on the fence plank and knocked it loose, dropping the one end to the ground. Tom jumped back with a "Whoa girl!" and reached a hand to the base of her neck as she turned with open mouth and tried to bite him. Tom attributed this uncharacteristic behavior from the mule to her propensity to stay in the barn, especially on cold days, and today was the coldest day of the winter. The temperature had dropped to twenty below zero and Tom had purposely waited till after sunrise to leave on his search. His first trip to the barn was to feed the animals and milk the cow, who was also a tad bit uncooperative and tried to kick over the milk pail. By the time Tom got back to the house, a thin film of ice already covered the usually warm milk.

After fighting with Meg to get her geared up, Tom finally pushed back to big door, led her through and slid the door closed. Tying her at the hitchrail below the porch, he mounted the steps and went to fetch the rest of his gear, the saddle bags and bedroll. He was purposely stalling, thinking there might be others that would show up to assist in the search, but when all was done, and no one came, he waved goodbye to Amy who was peering out the frosty window, choosing to stay in the warm house instead of standing on the porch to bid him goodbye. They had said their goodbyes with a hug and a kiss, and she was sending Tom off, wrapped in her prayers.

The frozen grass crunched beneath Meg's hooves, her breath already forming ice crystals on the few long hairs by her nose. Tom's scarf, wrapped around his neck and face, showed ice crystals just below his eyes and across that part covering his nose and mouth. He felt the piercing cold through the many layers of wool and shearling that was supposed to keep the cold at bay but was not doing its job. He hunkered down, feeling like a turtle drawing in its neck, and hunched his shoulders as he bent forward slightly.

When he looked up, a rare shaft of sunlight pierced the cloud cover and caught ice crystals floating in the air that sparkled their warning of frigidity. As they crossed the bridge, he glanced at the shallow river and saw it was frozen over, with one small patch of open water and steam rose from the warmer water only to be quickly turned to ice crystals and fall back into the opening. He knew by the time he returned, even that spot would be frozen over and he thought he wouldn't be surprised to see it frozen solid.

Tom's plan for the day was to go back to the place where they found Tommy's .22 rifle and start again. He would ride in circles around that point, and with each passing, increase the circle so that he could cover the entire hillside. Once that was done, he would move farther up the narrow draw, zig-zagging and comb the area, turning over every rock if he had to, but he wanted to make sure his son was not anywhere in this area. If unsuccessful, he would move to the next hillside tomorrow.

As he entered the trees, he was hopeful the sun would break through the dense cloud cover and bring a little warmth to the day and better light for the dark timber. But what he encountered were snow drifts with a top layer, melted the day before, but now frozen with a thick crust of hard frozen ice. As he dug his heels into the ribs of the recalcitrant mule, she would step forward, breaking through the crust and pushing the icy layer with her chest, another crunching step, and push again. It was hard going, every step a challenge, but Tom was determined and kept kicking and encouraging Meg forward. After about twenty minutes of fighting the crusted snow in the trees, they broke into a slight clearing and Meg stopped and blew, stomping her feet and bent her head around and looked as if to tell Tom to dismount.

He stepped down to the ground, looking around the small clearing, glad to be free of the snow drifts and stomped his feet and slapped his arms, trying to get the circulation going. He thought he had never been so cold, and he looked back at Meg, head hanging and breathing hard, the cloud of her breath showing ice crystals. He looked her over, ice crystals on her eyelashes, tiny icicles hanging from the long hair of her winter coat, and she shook, trying to rid herself of the ice. Tom stepped back, and something caught his eye, he bent to look at Meg's chest and saw blood. He dropped to one knee and reached out to examine her chest and saw several abrasions with the hair torn free and small cuts all across her chest. He reached out to examine them more closely and saw her legs were wounded in the same manner. He hung his head, reached up and stroked her neck and spoke, "I'm sorry

Meg, that was stupid of me, I shouldn't have done it, I'm sorry."

She had faithfully carried him the last several days, covering more ground in these days than she had traveled in the last couple of years, and now she stood, trembling slightly with blood slowly oozing from the wounds of faithfulness. Tom had learned as a youth to always be prepared when traveling in the mountains and he went to his saddlebags and pulled out a round tin of Watkins Petro-Carbo salve. It was the all-purpose remedy that most everyone had made their go-to aid for just about everything and everyone. He dipped his finger into the thick ointment and began applying it to Meg's wounds, smoothing it over the cuts and abrasions and stanching the flow of blood. When he finished, he stepped back and stroked Meg's face, talking to her and appeasing his own conscience.

———

IT WAS THE SMELL AS MUCH AS ANYTHING THAT brought him awake. He didn't want to open his eyes, he was warm and comfy, and he pinched his eyes shut and tried to snuggle back into the soft warm fur. But it didn't smell like his blankets and he didn't have any fur on his bed. He slowly opened his eyes and without moving, he looked around. But the darkness was all around and revealed nothing. He moved his head slightly, heard the sound of breathing and felt his bed or blanket or whatever it was, move a little. He drew in a deep breath, wrinkled his nose at the smell and looked around again. There was a glimmer of light over his head, but what he saw was grey rock like in a cave. A cave? He moved his head to the side just a fragment of an inch and looked towards the wheezing sound. His eyes grew large and he caught his breath, afraid to move. His heart began to beat so rapidly he thought it was going to come out of his chest.

He slowly let out his breath and moving only his eyes he looked again at the source of the sound, white teeth, long ones showed, and the edge of the lip fluttered with each breath. He didn't want to think it, didn't want to say it, but he was certain his furry pillow was a grizzly bear. He put his hand to his chest, certain that his heart was beating so loudly it would alarm the bear. He slowly moved to sit up, pushed away from the belly of the beast, felt the protrusion of bare skin and knew it to be one of several nipples, telling him this was a female grizzly. He looked around, fearful of seeing cubs and remembering his Pa saying the most dangerous place in the world was to be between a mama grizzly and her cubs. His eyes were becoming accustomed to the darkness and he saw no other balls of fur anywhere near and he breathed a little easier. But what was he to do? He looked back to his right at the source of the bit of light that bounced off the top of the cavern, but could see nothing, yet surmising that was the entrance and it was at least ten to twelve yards just to the bend in the cave, and he had no idea how far it would be to the opening.

He heard and felt a low growl, turned to look at the bear but there was no movement and then realized it was his own stomach. How long had he been here anyway? The last thing he remembered was crawling under the limbs of that big spruce and wanting to start a fire. But he leaned back against the tree and tried to get warm, he was so cold, and he must have fallen asleep. But how did he get here? He felt all over, he still had his coat and cap on, but as he took inventory of his gear, he was missing a mitten, but the bag with the biscuits was still tied to his wrist. He brought it to his lap, pulled open the draw strings and reached for a biscuit with apple butter.

He closed his eyes as he savored the biscuit and reached for another. As he pulled it out, he was startled by a cold nose touching his hand, the big face of the bear opened, and eyes looked at him as he froze in his motion. But a nudge from the black nose of the monstrous beast made Tommy offer the biscuit to the bear, who wolfed it down without chewing. The big bear sat back on its haunches, forelegs hanging in front of its massive belly and watched as Tommy reached for another biscuit. The boy slowly moved the biscuit to his mouth and shoved the whole biscuit in before the bear could take it from him. But the bear just watched. Maybe it was just that special connection, that affinity that children and animals enjoy but bear and boy seemed to instantly connect and trust one another. The big beast nodded his head and Tommy reached for another biscuit as the massive mouth leaned forward and open for its turn at the treats.

Tommy spoke, "My Pa and Ma will never believe me when I tell 'em I shared biscuits with a grizzly." The bear cocked his head to the side as Tommy spoke as if she understood his talking and seemed to smile at his remark. Tommy drew the strings on the bag and set it aside as he turned to face the big bear. He knew he should be afraid, even terrified, but there was something comforting about the presence of a friend, though a very furry friend it was. "Well, Mrs. Grizz, I don't think you're gonna eat me, otherwise you'da already done it, unless you was just waitin' for me to thaw out, but what am I gonna do? Are you gonna let me outta here?"

He slowly stood up, never taking his eyes off the big bear, and looked around at his new quarters. It was a cavern about twenty feet across and higher than Tommy could reach, but not as high as the ceilings in his home. He took a couple of steps toward the light, looked back at the bear and took a couple more. He wanted to see how far around that bend he would have to go to get to the opening of the cave. He thought if he just took his time, maybe the bear would think he wasn't really going anywhere and he could make it outta here.

Tom broke trail for Meg as he led her down the slope to the sunny side of the valley. There was a slight shoulder that was free of snow and brush and would be easier going. He could not continue his search through the hard-crusted snow and he knew he would have to wait until the weather warmed up enough to soften the crust, and the way this day was shaping up, all he could expect was the rest of the day and into the night, nothing but below zero temperatures and all that would do is make the crust even more difficult to break and find a trail. He knew Meg had given her all and he could not expect any more of the faithful mule, but some way, somehow, he had to continue his search. He couldn't stand the thought of his boy being out and lost in this kind of weather.

———

Pastor Davis walked to the balustrade railing and asked, "May I see J.B. Randall, please?"

The mousy clerk looked up at the well-dressed man

with a wool frock coat and a Homburg hat, forced a smile and asked, "Do you have an appointment, Sir?"

"No, I do not, but I am Mr. Randall's pastor and he asked that I stop in to see him," explained Pastor Davis, politely, as he removed his hat and stood ready to shuck his coat.

"I'll see if he can see you, sir. Excuse me," answered the clerk as he rose and motioned to the seats along the wall for the pastor to wait. The pastor turned and started for the seats but was stopped by the voice of J.B., "Pastor, good to see you. Won't you come in?" and opened the gate in the banister with a sweep of his hand to direct the pastor to his office, smiling broadly but with a touch of condescension in his eyes.

J.B. followed the pastor in to the president's inner sanctum and motioned him to the well-padded chair in front of the desk. "And to what do I owe this unexpected honor?" asked the portly president as he walked behind his desk and seated himself in the large, leather, reclining armed executive chair, that reminded the pastor of a king's throne. As he sat down and folded his hands across his vest and looked down at the pastor, he seemed to take great pride in his position that he deemed superior to everyone else.

"Thank you for taking the time to see me, Mr. Randall, I know you must be a very busy man," began the pastor, shrewdly flattering the man with such an evident overinflated ego. The rotund executive smiled and nodded his head. The pastor continued, "Mr. Randall, or may I call you J.B.?"

"Of course, pastor, of course, go ahead," he suggested making it a point of extracting his gold pocket watch, popping the cover open to look at the time, and with that move suggesting the pastor was on borrowed time.

"J. B., I have always been one to be frank and forthright and I wanted to ask you regarding this past Sunday and your lack of response regarding the Turner boy. Almost everyone turned out and either brought food, helped prepared things at the house, or went on the search themselves, but a few asked about you and were concerned you might not be feeling well." The pastor had carefully crafted his question to give the man an out with the illness option, then waited for his response.

"Well, well, blustered J.B. as he leaned forward, placing his elbows on the desk, "As you said, I am a very busy man and I just, well, I don't have time for every little concern that people have, after all."

"I would hardly consider a lost child a 'little concern' and it was the Lord's day, after all, and, well, you are the chairman of the Deacon Board and as such, people look to you as an example. Now, most everyone has spoken highly of you and how in times past you were one of the first to be there to help someone out. The congregation as a whole has held you in high esteem, but, I'm concerned, because lately, your actions have, frankly, not been the right example."

"Harummph, now, you wouldn't be listening to the gossip of some ne'er-so-wells would you pastor?" replied J.B. as he shuffled some papers on his desk but would not look at the pastor.

"J.B., I am equally concerned for everyone in my flock. And I do not listen to gossip. But I also know what it is to suffer a loss, like when you lost your son in the war, and the emotions that brings out."

The man jumped to his feet and leaned across his desk,

shook his finger in the pastor's face, "What would you know about losing a son? You pastor's think you know how everyone should feel and you get up on your high horse and preach about it. But let me tell you! The last thing you want to do is lose a son, and to top it off, have all these other sons come home to their families, but why couldn't God bring mine home? Huh? Answer me that!" He plopped back into his chair and swiveled it to the side, as if to dismiss the pastor.

The pastor dropped his head for a moment, thought back to when he and Rebekah had lost their two year old son to pneumonia, something that no one at this church knew, and then lifted his eyes to the hurting man and spoke softly, "Would it really have made you feel better if the other families lost their sons too? I'm certain there were many, many families that lost their sons, and some of them lost more than one. I know Tom Turner was in that same bottle, is that what has upset you so? Would it really make you feel better for Tom to lose his son?"

J.B. slowly turned back to face the pastor, took a deep breath, "It's not that pastor. I just had such plans for my son, how he'd take over the bank and all, and he had a sweetheart and we hoped to have grandchildren, and just like that!" he snapped his fingers, "it's all gone! I just can't get over it!"

"J.B., would you do something for me? Would you take just a moment and think about another father, a father that loved so much, he had his most precious and only son shed his blood so that others may have eternal life. Don't you think the Heavenly Father loved his son as much and even more than you loved your boy?" The pastor saw the president drop his shoulders and look down at his desk, silently and slowly nodding his head. "From what I understand, your son was a young man that was very involved in the church before he went to war, is that right?" Again, the older man nodded, but this time he lifted his eyes to the pastor. Pastor Davis said, "My guess is that before he left he said something about serving his country and protecting his homeland and probably something about duty? Is that right?"

J.B. lifted his head and smiled, "Yessir, he did. That was my boy, and I was very proud of him, too. He was so proud of that uniform and what he was going to do, I thought he'd pop some of those buttons right off that uniform. He was a fine boy!" He reached to the corner of his desk and turned a framed photo for the pastor to look at, it was just as the man described, a young proud soldier, shoulders back, chin up, and a smile of determination across his face.

"I would be just as proud. He's a handsome lad," said the pastor and looking up from the picture, leaned forward just a little, "J.B., this family has willingly given of their time. Tom to make sets for the Christmas program and Amy to play for it and help my wife with the children, and this in the midst of the hardest time of their lives. They are faced with losing their home, and yet they give of their time for the church. And now, think of this, they cannot take a breath without images of their little boy, out there in the wilderness and some of the worst weather we have had all year, and he could be freezing to death on a day like today. And worse still, there was sign that a grizzly bear might have taken the boy. Now, can you imagine the emotions that have been going through their minds and hearts?" He paused to look at the man before him, and the hardened expression that marked the man's face when first they met, now was replaced by just a hint of compassion.

J.B. looked up at the pastor, "A grizzly? Are you sure?

They're supposed to be hibernating and a grizzly hasn't been seen in this area in a long time."

"There was no mistaking the prints in the snow, it was a grizzly alright and where sign of the boy stopped, the grizzly tracks continued."

"What a horrible thought, a grizzly." He shook his head, then lifted his eyes to the pastor. "I guess I have been acting like a stubborn and selfish old fool. What can I do to help, pastor?"

"Well, as a church, we're going to have a grocery drive. It seems the boy knew about the money crunch his folks were facing and he went hunting, thinking he could help out by getting a deer. So, I believe we could at least do that much."

"Of course, of course. I'll have my wife pick up some things and we'll take it, uh, to the church?" he asked, hopeful.

"Well, yes. That would be fine. But there's more," he started but was interrupted.

"If you're thinking about me joining the search, I haven't been on a horse in years and I'm afraid I'd be more of a burden than a help."

"No, it's not that. Several of the men have joined Tom in his search. But because he has been out searching everyday and much of the nights, he hasn't been able to work. And since he can't work, I don't think they'll be able to make their payment," and again J.B. interrupted.

"Say no more, pastor. Tell them they don't have to worry about that payment, oh, until next year at this time. How's that?"

The pastor stood and extended his hand, "J.B., I had high hopes that you would see it in yourself to help, and I am greatly pleased. You are truly the example people said you were."

J.B. stood and extended his hand, smiled, and said, "I caught that 'you were' and I fully understand. I know I haven't been what I was, and I pray that God will allow me to become what I should be, in every way. Thank you, Pastor."

———

TOMMY SLOWLY MADE HIS WAY TO THE LIGHT, TRYING not to look back at the Mama grizz and to appear nonchalant, hoping he could slip out without her knowing. As he rounded the bend in the cavern, he stopped, mouth agape, as he looked at the entrance and saw nothing but snow. The light was able to shine through just enough to enable him to see, and as he looked, he thought it couldn't be too deep or the light wouldn't come through at all. He quickened his step thinking he was around the bend from the bear and could not be seen. What appeared as the opening was not much more than a slash in the rock and he dropped to one knee to reach out to touch the snow. He thought the opening was low, thinking that if it was open, he would have to bend over and maybe even crawl to get through. He thought about the bear and pictured the big beast having to practically belly down to get in and out.

Suddenly, the top edge of the snow mound seemed to crumble, and he looked up and reached out to scrape away some more snow. But whatever it was he was hoping for, he was disappointed to see several branches of juniper and pine that seemed to be crisscrossed over the opening. His first thought was that if his Pa was searching for him, there was no way he could see this opening behind that wall of branches. He dropped to his haunches and was startled when the big bear came up beside him and pushed at him with her head, directing him back into the cavern.

"You sure are pushy! Alright, alright, I'm going. I couldn't get out there now anyway." He reached in his coat pocket, felt another biscuit and pulled it out. He tore it in half and gave half to the bear and the two new friends walked together back to the place where she had bedded down with the boy. "But what am I gonna do for food? I'm about out of biscuits!"

WHEN AMY SAW THE LONE RIDER COMING ACROSS THE pasture at mid-day, she caught her breath, scraped the frost off the window with her fingernails and bent for a closer look. It was Tom, no mistaking that, but what was he doing back so early? She looked again, searching the figure for any sign of something or someone with him, but it was evident the man in the saddle was alone and the shuffling gait of the mule told her they were bearers of bad news. She clapped her hand to her mouth and sucked in a quick breath, thinking it must be about Tommy. Her breath came faster, and her heart seemed to skip a beat or two as she stood frozen before the window. Tom disappeared into the barn and soon re-appeared walking to the house, saddlebags over his shoulder.

Amy turned only her head as the door pushed open and a waft of cold air filled the room. Tom turned around, saw her by the window and her big eyes told him of her fear. "No, no, it's not what you think," he started as he stepped to take her in his arms, "I haven't found anything. It's just the cold and ice, I wasn't thinking and pushed Meg to the top of the ridge and she was cutting trail all the way, but the icy crust on the snow cut her up pretty bad and I had to bring her back. It was stupid of me, but I, well, I was just so focused on finding Tommy, I wasn't paying attention and she paid the price." He felt Amy relax in his arms and she nuzzled his chest, nodding her head, unable to speak until her emotions settled down.

"I'm glad you're back, for some reason I was more worried today than other days, it's just so cold out there," explained Amy, burying her face in his cold Mackinaw. She realized he still hadn't taken off his coat and she stepped back, "I'm sorry, you need to take off your coat. I'll put a couple slices of cornbread and some meat in the oven and we'll have lunch."

"Sounds mighty good to me! Is there any coffee left?"

"Ummhummm," said Amy, over her shoulder and pointed to the pot. "I'll get the cornbread and you can pour yourself a cup and while you're at it, pour me one as well."

As they sat at the table, Amy stretched out her hand to cover Tom's and asked, "Do you really think you might still find him?"

He looked down at the steaming coffee, lifted his eyes to hers and said, "Well, the way I see it is it's a good thing we haven't found anything yet, cuz that means he's still out there somewhere. But it's a bad thing cuz he's still out there and we don't know where. I think Tommy is a smart and resourceful boy and I'm hopin' he just got himself a hidey-hole somewhere and either can't get out, or maybe he's hurt, or something, but, yes, I believe we still have hope."

His expression was so somber and serious, Amy believed he truly believed there was hope. She breathed deep and said, "Oh, I hope you're right. You know I've been struggling with this, bein' mad at God and all, but I want to believe there's hope. I do, really, I do. But, it's been four, going on five days! And there's so many things that could happen. After all, it was just a few days back when you were attacked by a lion, and he's all alone." She dropped her head onto her arms and started crying, then lifted up to wipe the tears from her eyes. She sucked in a sobbing breath and looked to Tom. "You must think I'm a bawl baby!" And she wiped her tears and dripping nose.

He touched her shoulder and said, "I don't think nothing of the sort. You're a mother and you have every right to show your emotions, if you didn't, I'd really wonder about you!"

She forced a smile and stood, went to the stove to retrieve the coffeepot and refill their cups. Tom had finished his corn bread and meat and pushed his plate aside. "If you're going to be alright, I think I'll use this time to finish that project for the pastor."

"But, it's so cold out there," she pleaded.

"Ah, I'll start a fire in that ol' pot-belly and warm it up. I'll probably get it done in a couple hours anyway, but if you're so inclined, you can bring me out some coffee after a while." He grinned at his wife and she nodded her head as she touched her hanky to her eyes to catch a last tear.

She smiled as she thought, "That will be just fine. Because with school out, they're going to have a full practice of the program tomorrow morning, and you can give me and Tammy a ride into town in the morning when you haul that manger set for the program!"

"Alright, alright. I was kinda hopin' he'd have somebody come and get it, but I s'pose I can take it in to 'em. Then I'll come back and head to the hills cuz it'll probably be warmer then and maybe the crust on the snow'll be meltin'."

———

It was the scolding chuck-chuck and whistle from a whiskey jack perched on a limb by the cave opening that stirred Tommy awake. He was surprised he had slept, he was so hungry his stomach hurt. The last bit of biscuit and apple butter was eaten early yesterday and even though he didn't know what day it was, it seemed like it had been over a week since he had a good meal. As he lifted his eyes to the cavern ceiling, he was surprised it was so light. He turned to see the grizzly was sleeping soundly and carefully rose from his usual place with his head on her belly. She didn't stir, and he stood and looked around. The cave looked so much different, the light from the entry was brighter today and seemed to bounce around the walls of his prison. He noticed what appeared as crooked bands of white coursing along the wall behind the bear's bed and in the brighter light, they seemed to sparkle. He thought about how his Ma had talked about putting some pretty rocks around her flower beds and was sure she'd be pleased with this white rock that looked kind of like crystals.

The whiskey jack's shrill whistles and screams echoed through the cavern and startled Tommy, making him look to see if the bear stirred. But the mama grizz didn't even twitch. Tommy started tip toeing towards the entry to see what he could see and maybe figure out a way to get home. As he rounded the bend, he was surprised to see the opening was clear of snow and he quickened his pace for the last few yards, he bent low to see if he could clear the opening and stepped out of the cavern, scaring the whiskey jack into flight. He stood and froze in his tracks, surprised to see a wall of snow before him.

The wind in the mountains is a marvelous sculptor and

snow is its favorite medium. Although there was a bowl of emptiness before the cave entrance, the wall of snow had been sculpted with an overhanging cornice that was a little higher than Tommy could reach, even with his best flat-footed jump. The bright sun was almost blinding as it used the white of the snow to reflect its brilliance at the cliff wall that held the entry to the cave. The few trees and the brush that grew before the cave entry were free of snow, what with the warm sun and the reflected heat from the cliff wall, but the curved wall of snow seemed impervious to the warmth. Tommy walked to the snowbank, kicked at it and tried to get a foothold to climb, but the ice crust would not give way. The overhanging cornice shaded the undercut snow and it formed a literal ice wall that arched away from the cliff, offering no hope of escape.

Tommy kicked at the snow at his feet, looked back at the wall, and turned back to the cave's entry. Something caught his eye and he pushed past the branches of the juniper and saw a silver leafed bush, well protected by the cliff and the juniper. What snow there had been hadn't hardly curled the leaves, and the red that caught Tommy's eye showed several bunches of what Tommy recognized as buffalo berries. They were somewhat shriveled by the snow and cold, but he knew they were edible and he reached out to gather the harvest. One handful in his mouth, one in his pocket, one in his mouth and so on. The bitter berry had been mellowed by the cold but still made the boy pucker, but he was glad to have something to eat. He was amazed at the abundance, because this was one of the favorite foods of bears, and yet it appeared the bush hadn't even been touched. *Maybe Mama grizz was just savin' it for a mid-winter snack* he thought, grinning at his naming the bear, Mama grizz. He knew she would probably sniff out his berry harvest, but until then he would try to keep it to himself, even though that was being selfish.

When he entered the cave, his eyes went to the band of white rock on the wall and he walked nearer. With the brighter light, he saw the stone with veins of darker color coursing through and thought it would look pretty in his mother's flower garden. A smile stretched his face and he thought this would make a great Christmas gift for his mother. He ran his hand across the stone, wondered at the shiny parts and remembered his dad talking about Mica, and looked closer. But it had kind of a yellowish color and his next thought was of Iron Pyrite, or fool's gold. *That must be it, yeah, fool's gold. Pa said it kinda looks like gold but is just iron. But it makes the white rock look even prettier.* He tugged at a couple protrusions that had plenty of both colors and broke loose a few chunks. He had tucked the empty drawstring bag that carried his biscuits into his belt and now pulled it free. He sorted through the loose pieces of white rock, picked out what he thought were the prettiest, and filled his sack with four stones, each about the size of his fist. When he pulled the drawstring tight, he was surprised at the weight, but pictured his mother's smile when she saw the pretty rocks and grinned happily. *I just hope it stays warm and melts that snow a little. If it does, I can probably climb that drift and maybe get outta here, hopefully before Christmas.* He took a deep breath and unbuttoned his coat, having worked up a bit of warmth picking berries and digging rocks, walked to the little pool of water where the tiny trickle of water came from the crack in the wall, and got down on his belly to drink his fill.

He remembered talking to his Pa about the few experiences he had in the war that he would talk about and remembered him saying that a person could go ten or twelve days without food, but not more than two or three days without water. He was glad to have the water, and what little food he brought and found, but he hoped he wouldn't have to try to go much longer. He didn't think he could make it too much longer and he knew that Mama grizz wouldn't be too sympathetic.

THE PASTOR'S WIFE, REBEKAH DAVIS, AND DOROTHY
Leggitt from the Dress Shop were surprised to see the Turner's pull up to the church in the wagon loaded with wood-
work. Rebekah stood on the steps and said, "Why Amy, I
didn't really expect to see you today, but I'm awfully glad
you're here, and Tom, is that the manger set for the
program?"

Tom tipped his hat and answered, "Yes'm, it sure is. I'll
bring it in and get it set up if there's another man around to
help me get it unloaded and carried in."

"Of course, of course, my husband is just inside, I'll get
him." She turned and hurried back into the church building
as Tom and Amy climbed down from the wagon. Tammy
had already jumped down and ran inside with the other
children in the program.

With the help of Pastor Davis, the manger set was
unloaded, and Tom was busy at assembling the log pole
structure. "I like the way it looks, Tom, that bark on the
poles gives it a rustic look. I like it."

"Thanks Pastor. It's only because it was so cold

yesterday and Meg was stove up, so I couldn't search anymore, that I had time to get it done."

"Well, you've done a fine job and it'll make the program that much better. I'm very thankful for you doing this, what with everything else your dealing with right now. Have you made any progress in your search?"

Tom stopped his work and looked at the pastor, "No, pastor, I'm afraid not. Not even so much as another track. What with the snow and the cold, I just don't know." He lifted his head to return to drilling the holes for the wooden pegs, "but I'm not giving up. Not until I know for sure, I don't care if it takes the rest of my natural life. But for right now, I believe Tommy is just waitin' out there to be found. Maybe he's hurt, crippled up, or something, but I believe he's still alive."

"It's good to keep faith, Tom, and I will continue to pray for both of you."

"Well, I appreciate that pastor." He paused, looked at the floor and back at the pastor, "My Ma used to say there's a connection between a child and his parents. She told of other mothers knowing when their sons had died in battle even before they got word, they just knew. And I have this nagging in my soul that says Tommy's alive and I've got to find him." Tom stepped back from his work and said, "I think that'll do it. Think it's goin' to do the job?"

The pastor grinned and said, "Yessir, it'll do the job. And, thanks, Tom, thanks."

TOM LEFT TO RETURN TO HIS SEARCH AND THE WOMEN gathered the children around to start their last practice. "Samuel, since you're the narrator, we'll have you stand behind the pulpit. But first, we need to move it to the side over there," directed Rebekah. "Now, as soon as you're ready, begin."

"Yes'm," answered Samuel, the boy was big for his age, much like his father, the blacksmith, but he had a deep voice and was an excellent narrator as he began, "And it came to pass in those days..." When he came to the part, "...there was no room for them in the inn," he paused as directed.

"Very good, Samuel. Now, Cody, Clarissa, you come to the door and knock."

"But Mrs. Davis, Tommy's not here to answer the door. What should I do?" asked Eleanor.

"Well, we'll just have to let the innkeeper's wife do all the talking. But, if Tommy gets back, he'll do his part, understood?"

"Yes'm," replied Eleanor, as she looked at Clarissa who fancied herself as Tommy's girlfriend. The girls had been jealous of one another for as long as they had known each other, and now as they were approaching the age of interest in boys, that envy/jealousy had become more obvious. But Clarissa did not respond to Eleanor's glance and the practice continued.

The rehearsal of the dramatic parts and spoken parts went very well, but the music needed a little work, so Amy took over the rehearsal and worked out all the musical numbers for the shepherds and the combined children's choir. Once the music part was acceptable, Rebekah asked for a complete rehearsal to include all the music. Everything went well, and Rebekah was lavish with her praise, eliciting broad smiles from each of the children.

As the practice was completed and the children gathered up their coats and caps, Rebekah asked Amy, "Could we give you a ride home? It's still quite chilly outside and you've a long way to walk."

"Thank you, Rebekah, that would be wonderful. I was hoping someone would offer, that road is getting quite muddy with the weather turning warmer and melting everything."

ONCE BACK IN THE BARN, TOM UNHARNESSED THE horses and led the big bay gelding to the corral fence and saddled up. He tied the bay to the hitchrail in front of the house and went in to restock his saddle bags with eats and coffee. Within moments, he was headed across the pasture and pointed to the valley of the little Cochetopa creek.

The weather had warmed considerably, and Tom looked at the clear blue sky and the sun shining unhindered upon the patchy snow. He knew the snow in the timber would be deeper and more difficult to traverse, but he also knew the warmth would have melted the crust and make it easier on both man and horse. He knew if he was able to ride the ridge of the mountain that shadowed the east bank of the Cochetopa, he could also look down on the draw near where they found Tommy's .22. That was the ridge and draw that had stopped him and Meg the day before but with the warm bright sun, he might be able to use his binoculars and search both slopes from atop the ridge. He didn't really expect to see much this far from where they first saw Tommy's sign, but he still had to give it another look.

He was right in his estimation of the snow condition, but as the warmth melted the snow, the ground around became muddy and boggy. But Tom pushed the big bay to take the known trail up the lesser ridge, knowing it would tie up to the top and with its bald slopes and exposure to the sun, it should be easy going. He was hopeful of topping out before stopping for his lunch.

The bay was winded after his hard climb, often crow-hopping through the deeper snow, but when they topped out and he saw some bunch grass and other tundra growth, he was glad when Tom picketed him and loosened the cinch. Tom slipped the saddle bags from behind the pommel and went to a sunbaked boulder to take up his vigil. As he sat cross-legged, he dug into the saddle bags and pulled out his dish towel wrapped leftovers, grinning in anticipation of sinking his teeth into the cold chicken leg. While he ate, he searched every ravine, every slope, every cluster of trees for any sign of movement or anything that might bring just the slightest hope. But all he saw were patches of white in splotches of dark green.

He finished the chicken leg, tossed the bones at a camp-robber whiskey jack that flapped his wings to jump back and spoil Tom's aim, and wiped his hands on the dish towel Amy had made from a flour sack. He reached for a chunk of cornbread and took a big bite, then movement caught his eye. He craned around trying to see more, as hope began to grow within, wanting to see something that told of his son. He grabbed at the saddle bags and pulled out the binoculars and scanned the area where he thought he saw movement. It had been something of a different color than the trees, maybe grey or brown, but he was certain he saw movement. He looked, stood and walked to the edge of the ridge and looked again, moving the binoculars slowly and searching. He dropped to his haunches, pulling his knees up to rest his elbows on and stabilize the binoculars. But try as he might, he could see nothing.

He dropped the binoculars down, and looked, then something black, but it was above. Buzzards! Turkey buzzards, several of them, circling! Something was dead, or about to be! He knew the carrion eaters could sense when something was dying and struggling, and they would circle and wait. What if it was...? No! He lifted the binoculars again, but saw nothing, too many trees. He rose, grabbing his saddle bags, and let the binoculars hang around his neck. The big bay lifted his head as Tom approached and dropped his head as Tom reached to tighten the girth.

Tom was filled with hope and despair. What if it was Tommy and he was too late? He gigged the bay and pointed him toward a ridge that led to the bottom and the narrow valley of the Little Cochetopa creek. Where the buzzards were circling was farther up the valley and the quickest way to get there was along the creek bottom.

The bay picked his footing, sometimes dropping his haunches underneath to slide down the steep slope with his front legs stiffened out in front to slow the slide. Tom was leaning back to put his weight on the rear end and to help the animal keep his balance, but he was anxious to get to the scene of whatever was in trouble before it was too late. He kept seeing images of his boy, struggling in the snow, fearful of what was happening and wondering where his father was, *Hang on son! I'm coming! Lord, if that's Tommy, protect him, please!* He let the big bay have its head and pick his own route through the snow and the trees, the animal sensed Tom's urgency and was doing his best to find the quickest way to the bottom.

When they cleared the trees at the bottom of the narrow valley, he turned the horse's head to the upper end of the valley and dug heels into the horse's ribs. There was still snow, but only about a foot deep and softened by the warm sun, but the bright sun was almost blinding as it reflected off the snow. Tom kicked him up to a canter and the big bay lunged forward.

Suddenly, Tom saw movement at the tree line, and grabbed for his rifle. He thought he saw a wolf, black or dark grey, but it was just a fleeting glance. Then he thought of whatever was down and was fearful that it was Tommy and a wolfpack had attacked. The bay kicked at the snow with every lunge and they were closing the gap quickly. Tom looked to the sky and saw the still circling buzzards and it looked like there were more than before. His heart was booming in his chest and ears and his breath was coming in great gasps, his eyes wide as he leaned along the neck of the bay as the mane whipped in the wind. *I've got to get there in time!*

As he drew near and rounded the point of trees, he pulled back on the reins and the bay dropped his rear to slide to a stop in the snow. Something was already down, and three wolves turned to look, fangs bared and eyes glaring from slits, at this new intruder. Although Tom couldn't hear it, he knew they were growling. As he swung a leg over the rear of the horse, he saw something brown and bloody on the ground by the wolves. He remembered his boy had a brown coat with a fur collar, and Tom's anger flared. In an instant, he brought the rifle to his shoulder as he jacked a shell into the chamber, and as soon as he had a wolf in his sights, he quickly squeezed off his first shot. Before the boom of the bullet quit echoing between the hills, another shot sounded and another, so fast it was like rolling thunder. One wolf was down and kicking, another had been burned on his rump and was running with his tail tucked between his legs and the other stood his ground even after a bullet plowed snow between his feet. He took a threatening step towards Tom but was met with the slug from the .25-35 rifle that Tom's dad had named the Coyote Killer.

Tom jacked another shell into the chamber but lowered the rifle as the threat of the wolves was gone. He walked slowly toward the carcasses, cautious about the wolves, not knowing if they were dead or just wounded, but also fearful of what he was going to find. He heard his own feet crunch in the snow, heard the whisper of the wind through the trees, high above he heard the screech of a red-tailed hawk, and over it all was the thunder in his own chest.

He kept his eyes on the wolves, watching for any telltale sign of life, poking each one with the rifle barrel to ensure they were dead. After he was certain they were not a threat, he slowly turned his eyes to the object of their gluttony and let a long breath escape as he saw the legs and hooves of an elk. It was the carcass of a yearling, light brown hair with the dark hair at its neck that made Tom think of Tommy's coat. He dropped to his knees, weak from the fight and the surge of adrenalin, and relieved it wasn't his son. But the realization of how easily it could have been Tommy began creeping back into his consciousness and he stood and walked back to the big bay. As he looked at the big gelding, sides heaving with exhaustion, white lather showing under the martingale and the edges of the saddle, he realized, once again, he had pushed a faithful animal beyond reason. He spoke softly as he approached the blaze faced head of the horse, reached out and rubbed the horse's forehead and cheeks, and patted it on the side of the neck as he dropped his own forehead to rest against the white blaze on the horse's forehead.

He despised anyone that mistreated animals, especially horses and mules that served their owners so faithfully, and here he had become exactly what he scorned in others. He slipped the rifle into the scabbard and picked up the reins and started walking through the snow following the trail his horse had broke on the way up. He would lead the horse to let it catch its wind, and maybe all the way back to the barn. He hung his head in shame at his foolishness and determined never to do it again. But in his heart, he also knew he would not give up the search, no matter the cost. But tomorrow was Christmas eve, and he had a difficult choice. Should he stay at home with Amy and Tammy, or should he try to search again?

As he walked, he remembered the sounds and scenes of battle. Some of the most gruesome images were those that had horses being beaten to pull cannon and wagons, others that were used by the cavalry and ridden into the face of murderous fusillades of entrenched soldiers. Every time he saw a horse fall he felt as much for the animal as he did for any of his fellow soldiers. His youth had been spent aboard a horse and they were always part of his life and those that have never had that special bond with an animal cannot understand the kinship between horse and rider.

They had come most of a mile before Tom mounted again, but he reined the horse back toward home and the warm barn and hay. He dropped the reins on the bay's neck and let him have his head and lowered his head and spent the next half hour just talking with the Lord. He had much to be thankful for, but his heart was heavy for his son and he thought about his Heavenly Father and understood just a little better what a sacrifice He had made when He sent His only Son to die on the cross. He lifted his head to see Amy sitting on the porch, watching the sun paint the western sky with bold stripes of crimson and orange. He saw her stand, arms folded, as she leaned against the porch post and waved at her returning husband. Once again, Tom thanked the

Lord for giving him such an understanding and wonderful wife. He knew he couldn't have made it this long if it weren't for her faith and faithfulness. Yes, even with everything else going on in his life, he was still a very lucky and blessed man.

WHEN HE PULLED ON THE TRUNK OF THE FRESH-CUT tree to squeeze it through the door, the outstretched branches seemed to grab hold of the door jamb to resist the efforts of the well-intentioned father and husband. Suddenly the spring-loaded branches folded in on themselves and the tugging Tom fell on his rear and the tree landed on top of him to complete the picture of humiliation. But that image wasn't enough, Amy and Tammy stood by the table, bent over with laughter at the Paul Bunyan of the Rockies, not unlike the one told about in the pamphlets of the Red River Lumber company. Only this lumberjack wasn't nearly as big as the one in the pamphlets and there was no blue ox waiting outside.

It felt good to laugh, and even better to laugh together. For a brief moment, worries, concerns, fears, and questions had been wiped aside and the tears that flowed were tears of joy and relief. Amy sat back in the chair, pulled Tammy close and they laughed again as they watched Tom struggle out from under the blue spruce that was destined to decorate their living room. Once free, Tom stood, dusted off the short blue needles and the left-over snow, and chuckled at his family, still giggling and laughing at his acrobatic entrance.

"Well, the least you could do is pour a man a cup of coffee to warm-up a little. After all, I've been roaming the woods looking for just the right tree since, well, early. And it's still winter outside, and your loving husband needs to warm up a little before I set that man-eating tree up for you to decorate." He took off his mackinaw and sat down in the chair opposite his wife and rested his forearms on the table, grinning at his girls.

Amy went to the stove to fetch the coffeepot, poured them both a cup, and as she sat down she pointed to the closet in the hall, "Tammy, there is a box in the closet that has some decorations of your grandparents. How 'bout you getting it out so we can get started on the tree?"

Tammy jumped up from the floor where she had been playing with some wooden toys that had been Tommy's and were passed down to her just last year. Amy watched her daughter run to the closet and turned her eyes to her husband, "It's so hard, not having Tommy here. Everything, just everything, tells of his absence." She put her hand to her mouth, struggling not to cry and Tom reached for the other hand, taking it in his and was reminded how tiny and frail his wife really was, and squeezed it for reassurance. That simple gesture said more than he could find the words to say as he dropped his eyes and lifted the cup to his lips, watching the steam rise from the hot brew.

"C'mon daddy! Let's get the tree up, so we can start decorating."

"Boy, you sure are bossy for such a little girl!" he declared then turned to his wife, "Do you women start teaching the girls this bossiness when they're this young?"

Amy slapped at Tom's shoulder, laughing at his sugges-
tion. "No, it just comes naturally. We don't have to be
taught!" Then stuck her tongue out at him, smiling and
giggling.

While Tom fashioned the tree stand with some lumber
scraps, Amy and Tammy strung fresh popcorn on a string,
interspersed with cranberries for color. Last night they had
fashioned bows from scrap material from the program
costumes and some ribbons were made into braided
garland. When Tom stood back, adjusted the tree, and
looked to Amy for her opinion, she smiled and gave him a
thumbs up of approval.

He stepped back from the tree and sat down at the
table, lifted his eyes to his wife and started, "I'm going..." but
she held up her hand to stop him.

"I know, we'll do the tree and get ready for the program.
Just try to get back in time to take us there if you can.
Please?" she asked, and she touched his shoulder gently.

"You know I will, but..."

"I know, and I would go with you if I could."

THE LONG-LEGGED MULE STEPPED OUT ANXIOUSLY,
showing her distaste for the barn as she tossed her head and
pulled at the reins. The cuts had all been minor and were
already scabbed over and starting to heal and the strong-
willed mule acted like she was five years younger than her
actual age of fourteen. But even though Meg was enthused
about their ride bound for the mountains, Tom was in more
of a melancholy mood. He looked at the cattle in the far
pasture, remembering his father's hopes for a bigger herd.
He stood in his stirrups as Meg crossed the bridge and he
scanned the entire ranch property, back yonder were the

buildings, the house, barn, corrals, tack shed, smokehouse, and root cellar. The big trees that surrounded the buildings formed an excellent windbreak and he remembered helping his Pa thin out the cottonwoods and the ponderosas, making room for their planned structures that now stood as a mute monument to those hopes and dreams. Beyond the fence lay the other 160 acres that Tom had filed and proved up on, and in the trees beyond the little river, the skeleton frame of their dream house he put up before he left for the war.

He dropped back in the saddle and let Meg have her head, knowing she could blindly take them to the corner gate, and thought about what they would have to do when they lost the ranch to the banker. His adjoining acreage and the start of the house were not included on the bank loan, but the house wasn't far enough along for them to live in, that would take weeks if not months, and then only if he could come up with enough money for the lumber and other supplies.

Meg had stopped and was waiting for Tom when he finally realized he was expected to open the gate. He leaned down and lifted the wire loop and picked up the end pole of the gate and gigged Meg through. Reining her around and backing her up alongside the gate, he replaced the end pole and dropped the loop over the top to secure the gate, all without leaving the saddle. He refocused his attention on his search and pointed Meg to the wide alluvial fan and on towards the wide mouth of the ravine where the two run-off draws joined. His plan was to return to the site where Tommy's .22 was found and look again at the lay of the land, just to see if he could determine where the grizzly might have gone. Maybe he could find the hibernation lair of the bear and some sign of Tommy. He knew he was thinking that the bear had probably taken the boy and all he would find might be a coat or something, but at least he would know.

He lifted his eyes to the cobalt canopy and unbuttoned his mackinaw as he lifted his face to the warm sun. It was still a cold winter day and oftentimes these clear sunshiny days could be deceiving, but not this day. Compared to the recent days of bitter bone-chilling below zero temperatures, this was like a spring day under the bright sun and clear sky. Tom sucked deep of the crisp clear air and used knee pressure to point Meg to the left fork of the ravines. It was on the west slope where the random spruce grew where Tommy had taken shelter, but it took a little searching to find the right tree. Things were considerably different than the snowy day he disappeared, but patches of snow remained and in the shaded ravine, drifts were still quite deep.

As he pushed through the usual juniper and piñon, he was suddenly confronted by the cluster of spruce and knew he found the right place. He reined up by the big gray barked spruce whose branches were spread wide, unlike that day when they hung low under the weight of the heavy snow, and he dropped to the ground to look around. The snow wasn't the pristine white of new fallen snow, but was littered with pine needles, an occasional cone, and looked like lonesome waifs as each drift remnant had to lay by itself in the shade of the spruce and pine.

Tom walked closer and bent under the wide branch to look at the spot by the big trunk where Tommy had sought shelter and protection. He dropped to one knee and looked around, searching for anything of his boy, but saw nothing. He hung his head as he turned and mounted Meg and once in the saddle he sat looking around. He gigged the mule forward between the two spruce trees and looked at the slope before him. He saw what appeared to be a bit of a saddle in one of the long ridges that pointed to the bottom of the draw and looking beyond and with a great deal of imagination, he could see a bear taking that route, if it wanted to get to the bottom of the ravine for some reason.

Tom clucked the mule forward and pointed her to the saddle as he searched the hillside around him. They crossed over the saddle of the ridge and started down the gulley between the ridges. Suddenly Meg stumbled and fell to her knees in the deep snow, catapulting Tom over her head and into the unexpected deep drift across the cut. He went head first into the snow and found himself buried in the granular white, head down and feet kicking against the looser snow at the top. With considerable effort, he pulled his arms forward and pushed the snow away from his face. He spit snow from his mouth, wiped it away from his eyes and nose and gulped deep breaths. He began pushing and kicking, trying to right himself and find the surface, finally getting his weight off his shoulders, he knelt in the small cavern he had formed with all his pushing and shoving. When he straightened up, he looked overhead and saw the blue sky and the big opening above. He pawed at the snow, pulling it down and beside him, pulled again and again. He stopped, and rested just a couple of moments, then began his swimming motions again and shortly had head and shoulders above the snow. He looked around and saw Meg standing patiently by, well away from the drift and on solid ground, giving him that look that made him think she thought he was stupid.

It was a little less than a quarter hour before he stood beside his mule and rested his head on the saddle, mustering up the energy to get mounted. "You know, Meg, maybe you're right, maybe, just maybe now, I am stupid. If I had been paying attention, I would have seen that drift and known it was too deep to go through." He mounted up and started the mule down to the bottom of the draw to look for any possible caves or other probable hibernation holes. When they bottomed out, they were in snow that was still about a foot and a half deep. He stood in his stirrups to see up the ravine but saw only deeper drifts that would prevent them from going much further. In his desperation, he cupped his hands to his mouth and called out, "Tommy! Tommy! Where are you boy? Tommy!" He dropped into the saddle, listened, and not a single bird could be heard only the whisper of the winter wind through the pines and down the valley. He pulled out his Pa's pocket watch and saw the time and knew he best head back to the house to take his girls to the program. He kept Meg out of the bottom of the draw, but they still had to push through deep snow to get out of the narrow valley. Once clear, Meg quickened her step, now anxious to return to the barn she had earlier spurned.

Tom unhitched the team and turned them into the corral, pulled the gate shut and followed Franklin Forrester into the church building. Most everyone was already seated, and the children had gathered in the two side rooms beside the choir platform, occasionally cracking a door to peek out at the crowd. Once everyone was seated, the pastor stepped to the front and raised his hands for silence. "Good afternoon everyone. What a joy it is to see so many of our community out on this wonderful Christmas Eve. Our children have worked very hard to present you the story of Christmas and under the guidance of my wife, Rebekah," and he paused as the crowd gave a smattering of applause, "and Dorothy Leggitt," again some applause, "and our pianist, Amy Turner," and more applause. "We are pleased to present to you, The Christmas Story." The pastor stepped aside and took a seat with others on the first row while Amy played a soft introductory number.

Samuel began his narration, "And it came to pass..." and while he spoke, the shepherds took their place, wrestling with two small lambs and their shepherd's crooks, but were seated by the time Samuel said, "And there were in the same country, shepherds... keeping watch over their flock." As he paused, Tammy stepped to her place on a wooden box, raised her hands and said, "Behold, I bring you good tidings of great joy... for unto you is born this day... a savior, which is Christ the Lord! And... ye shall find the baby, uh, uh, wrapped in swaddle cloths, in a manger." She knew she had missed a couple of words, but she smiled prettily, and everyone forgot right away.

With a single two-handed chord from the piano, the rest of the cast burst out in song singing "Glory to God in the highest, and on earth, peace, good will to men."

The program went very well, with the only hiccup being when the innkeeper's wife, Eleanor, was asked for a room by Joseph and she responded, "Uh, the innkeeper's not here, he's lost, but you can stay in the manger with the animals." When she said lost, many of the women especially, looked toward Amy and saw her drop her head, put her hand to her mouth, and wipe her tears.

At the conclusion of the program after the shepherds left, and Joseph and Mary picked up the bundle representing the baby and walked off the platform, the crowd stood to their feet and applauded enthusiastically. The pastor stepped to the platform and again raised his hands as everyone seated themselves again.

"As we think of Christmas, we must remember that it is not just a baby in the manger that we gather together for, but the birth of our savior, the Lord Jesus. He came, not just to be born in a manger, but to die on the cross, and He did that for you and for me. He paid a debt he did not owe for us who owed a debt we could not pay. You see, my friends, it's not just a time for Christmas trees and presents, but a time to remember that God sent His only Son so that we might have eternal life. And the way we have that eternal life, is to accept the greatest gift ever given. The gift of salvation, to be saved from the price of our sin, which is death and hell forever, and to receive the gift that grants us an eternal home in Heaven. So, as you gather together with your family around the tree this Christmas, don't forget the greatest gift. If you have never received it, please do so before this Christmas time is over." He stepped back and waited while Amy played softly on the piano, giving everyone an opportunity to go to the front and meet with the pastor.

When the invitation time was over, the pastor again stood before the crowd, "There is one more thing we must do before we leave. As you know, we have been praying for the Turner family and helping as we could. Little Tommy is still missing, but we haven't given up hope and, in the meantime, many of you have asked what else we could do to help. Now, unknown to Tom and Amy, while I was speaking, our deacon's have been loading the Turner's wagon with our gifts and they have brought it around front for them." The crowd stood to their feet and applauded as Tom went to stand beside Amy and Tammy. "So, Tom, Amy, you folks go ahead on out, we don't want to embarrass you, but we want you to know we love you and are praying for you."

With bowed heads and tears freely falling, Tom, Amy and Tammy walked down the center aisle and out the door to their wagon where J.B. Randall and John McPherson stood, holding the team and waiting. When Tom came down the steps, J.B. approached with his hand extended and as Tom grasped it, J.B. spoke, "Tom, forgive me for the way I spoke when we were at the bank. I was wrong, and I want you to know, we'll not be foreclosing, but you take all the time you need, even if it's a year or so, you folks have your home and it's safe."

Tom stifled a sob, grasped J.B.'s hand and nodded his head as he struggled to speak, "Thank you J.B., thank you. You don't know what this means. I'll not forget it. Thank you!" Tom turned to Amy, helped her up to the seat where Tammy sat waiting. He climbed up and nodded to the men, "Thank you. And tell everyone, thank you so much!"

"We will, we will. But I'm sure they already know. You do your best to have a Merry Christmas now folks," answered John, lifting his hand to wave goodbye to the family.

Tammy sat between her parents and they snuggled together beneath the wool patch quilt. Tammy asked, "Did I do O.K. Mommy?"

"You were wonderful, Tammy, absolutely wonderful! Don't you think so, honey?" she asked Tom.

"Why, you were the best angel in the whole program!"

"Daddy, I was the only angel!" she declared.

"Well, you were the best angel I've ever seen, then, how 'bout that?"

She smiled up at her Pa and said, "Alright," and crossed her arms in front of her, satisfied.

They rode toward the slowly setting sun and marveled at the way the rays shone like swords of light, each a slightly different color, as the sun dropped below the distant silhou-etted mountains. Each one of those on the wagon seat shared the same silent thought visible in their glassed over eyes, that it would be a wonderful Christmas eve, if only Tommy was here.

———

He kicked at the towering snowbank, testing the hardness of the crust of ice. It gave way and he was elated and hopeful and began digging at the small hole. He began fashioning a foothold, thinking he could make enough of them and climb up over the overhanging cornice and escape. He kicked again, but this time it was more difficult because he had to kick higher, but he cracked the crust, and dug again. Now he had two footholds, but when he tried to kick again, it was too high. He stepped back and looked, then turned around and kicked back with the heel of his boot, success! In a moment, he had three footholds and he stepped back again to look at his handiwork. He visually measured the footholds, the height of the drift wall, and wondered how he could make more. He walked closer, beat on the crust with his fist, but it hurt his hand and he drew back. Looking up at the sky and the warm sun that was already dropping to the west, he hoped it would be enough sunlight to melt the crust a little more, but he knew that once the sun dropped below the treetops, it would cool off and probably freeze again.

He looked around for anything he could use as a tool or something, there, that rock! He picked it up and hefted it, just right. And he went back to work on his prison wall of ice. With repeated bashings, he broke through the slightly thicker crust, and soon fashioned another foothold. But all that kicking, and digging was making him tired. He had eaten the last of the berries and hadn't had anything but water since this morning. His stomach growled as if on cue and reminded him he was quite hungry. He sat down on a nearby rock and looked at the wall. He saw that it curved back toward him the closer to the overhanging cornice, and he thought that if he did climb up those footholds, how would he get over the top?

He hung his head in discouragement and wondered if he was ever going to get home. He thought of his Mom and Dad and sister, wondering what they were doing now. He wasn't sure what day it was, but if it was getting close to Christmas eve, they were probably practicing the program. Or maybe just sitting at home having one of Ma's pot roasts with potatoes and carrots and onions and gravy. Boy, would he like some of that now!

The shadows stretched across the drift and drove Tommy back into the cave. The wind, once the sun was down, was too cold to stand out there and take. It seemed to blow right over that drift and up against the cliff face and even poke into the cavern some, but it was sure enough getting cold. He stealthily moved back into the cave and crawled up next to Mama Grizz and sought the warmth of her fur and soon dropped off to sleep, hopeful he would at least have a good dream.

Tom leaned his head against the warm flank of Bossy as he mindlessly pulled and squeezed to fill the milk pail. His left leg bent to trap the tail of the cow to keep her from whipping his face as she munched on the grain in the bin. A cry from the cat caught his attention and he squirted her mouth full of warm milk. The yellow tabby sat back on her haunches, flicked her tail around her front paws and cocked her head to the side as she waited for another ration of warm goodness. Tom took aim and squeezed off a white stream that painted the tabby's face before he hit the mark of the pink target of the cat's mouth. He grinned at the cat as she licked her face and chest, making sure not a drop was wasted. Tom remembered watching Tommy have fun with the cat from the time it was a kitten and he began teaching it to beg for milk.

He focused on the bubbles and foam in the pail as he continued the chore, but his mind went to the mountains, mentally reviewing every place he searched, trying to think of any spot that he might have missed. He had often wondered if he should expand his search but couldn't believe that Tommy could have gone any further, especially in the storm when he was lost. He was reminded of his Pa telling about a time they had searched for one of their neighbors, a recent arrival from the east, who was lost during a hunt for elk. The men of the village had searched for days before they found the man's body, well over five miles farther away than they thought he could have traveled on foot. His Pa had explained, "When somebody knows they're lost, they go into a panic and go farther and faster than you might think. And when they're turned around, why, they'll run for miles thinkin' they're gettin' closer t'home when they're really getting' farther away." Tom knew that was the nature of man, but the storm was a big factor and the boy couldn't buck the deep snow. After all, they had found his rifle and the boy wouldn't knowingly leave that behind. And he didn't really want to think about the possibility of the grizzly and what might have happened with a monster of the mountains like that.

Tom shook his head, checked each of the teats for milk, and satisfied he was finished, grabbed the pail and stood up to leave. He sat the pail on the workbench, released Bossy from the stanchion and started for the house. The sun was sending its lances of light above the eastern horizon to announce the new day and Tom turned to look as the low-lying clouds caught the colors of morning and as he watched, he softly recited, "Red sky at night, sailor's delight, red sky at morning, sailor's take warning." But there was only gold and orange announcing this day yet there were clouds, some with grey bottoms, that told of the possibility of snow, and for whatever reason, he knew a lot of folks liked the idea of a white Christmas. He smiled as he turned toward the porch.

He knew Amy would be puttering in the kitchen, fixing

a special breakfast for Christmas morning and Tammy would be anxiously waiting, probably sitting on the floor by the tree looking at the presents. When he pushed open the door, Tammy was standing, waiting, with her arms folded and her bottom lip pushed out, "Papa, there aren't any presents with my name on 'em!"

Tom sat the pail on the counter, turned to pick up his girl and said, "Well, maybe that's because they're still hidden away from your prying eyes, you little nosy girl you!" He pinched her nose to make her squirm.

"And there's no presents for Tommy, either?" she answered, still pouting in disappointment.

"Well, let's have breakfast before we go worrying about presents and such," interjected Amy. "Now, everybody get to the table before breakfast gets cold!"

———

WHEN TOMMY ROSE TO HIS FEET, MAMA GRIZZ stirred, but didn't waken, and the boy tiptoed to the cave entrance to see the colors of the morning reflected on the remaining snow. As he stepped from the cave, pushing aside the branches of the juniper and oak brush, his eyes grew wide when he saw the cornice of the snow had fallen and the wall of his snow prison had melted and was now no more that four feet high. He ran to the drift and kicked at it, pleased to see it was soft and mushy. He scrambled up the soft wall, slipping and digging with his one mittened hand. As soon as his eyes could see over the top, he froze in place, looking down the long sloping drift to see the bottom of the draw full of snow. He turned to look along the side of the mountain and knew that would be the way he would go. There was still a lot of snow and what appeared as deep drifts, but the trees were scattered, and the sun had done its work to melt away a lot of the deeper snow from the hillside. Tommy wondered if he could make it through such deep snow, but he knew he had to try.

He started to climb over the drift, but realized he had left his bag of rocks that held his mother's Christmas present, back in the cave with his cap. He looked back at the cave entrance, and back at the hillside that beckoned, but decided to retrieve the bag. As he neared the entrance, he took a deep breath, and bent at the waist to move back into the opening. He paused as he stood up, letting his eyes adjust to the semi-darkness, then stealthily walked back to his bed near the bear. He bent to pick up his cap and the bag, barely breathing, watching the big bear. She had rolled to her back, her head turned away, and forepaws bent over her chest, rising and falling with each deep breath that elicited a slight snore that made her lips flap with each exhale. Tommy looked at the beast, surprised he felt a touch of sadness at leaving her, then turned to tiptoe away.

With only one glance over his shoulder as he walked around the bend in the cave, he quickened his pace to be free of the cavern. Once again, pushing aside the branches, he stepped into the light of early day. He lifted his eyes to the sky and saw the many clouds of white and gray that appeared as if smeared by the Creator's brush and he felt the warmth of the sun although it was yet to show its face over the mountain ridge. He tied his bag of rocks to his belt, dropped his coat tail over the bag, and started pushing his way up the big drift. His hand had just reached the top when his feet started slipping in the mushy snow and he started to turn to see where to place his feet, when he felt something on his rump and he was suddenly pushed over the top!

He landed face first in the snow, but as he scrambled to get up, he started rolling down the steep white slope, over and over and over. He surprised himself when he hollered, flailing his arms to stop his rolling and kicking at the snow to slow his descent. Finally, he rolled up against a rise in the drift and was able to sit up, wiping his face and his body free from the wet and granular snow. He looked around to see where he landed and saw the big brown grizzly slipping and sliding down the slope toward him, big mouth open wide, eyes almost as wide, and claws and paws grabbing for a hold to stop. She came to a stop within arm reach of Tommy and quickly rolled to her belly and rose up on all fours, shaking her head and rolling her hide to shake off the excess snow.

Tommy started laughing at the antics of the bear, not thinking she might be after him and he could be in danger. But she was funny. Tommy stood, brushed himself off and turned to look for the best way to start home. He took a couple of steps and sunk in the deep snow up to his waist and his heart seemed to skip a beat. In that instant, his fear of not getting home seemed to overwhelm him and he dropped his head and wanted to cry, but he bit his lip, determined to free himself and get off this mountain.

Mama Grizz looked at the boy, floundering in the snow, and did exactly what she would have done if Tommy had been one of her cubs. She stretched out and caught the boy's collar in her teeth and jerked him up out of the hole and sat him down beside her. She looked at him, sniffed at him, and started to walk away, took two steps and looked back at the boy as if to say, "Well, come on!" and Tommy stood, caught a handful of fur and followed alongside the big bear with huge padded paws that kept her on top of the deep snow. Tommy struggled a bit, but with a firm grip on the thick fur on Mama Grizz' hip, he kept up the ambling pace, only slipping a few times, dropping into the deeper snow once, but he managed.

———

"Mama, did you make enough pancakes for Tommy?" asked the sincere little blonde with bouncing curls over the sober face.

Amy took a deep breath, struggling not to choke up, forced a smile and said, "We always have enough for everybody. You just get busy on your stack there or you won't get to open any presents," admonished her mother.

Amy had made their favorite blueberry syrup when they harvested the few wild blueberries they found in the fall and it was saved for special occasions and it couldn't be any more special than Christmas. Tom drenched his stack of pancakes with the syrup, handed it to Amy and watched as she did the same. When Amy started to pour some on Tammy's, the girl said, "No, Mommy, I want to do mine like Tommy always does his. I want apple butter!" Amy looked at the girl, surprised, and asked, "But you always have syrup?"

"Uhhhuh, but today I want it like Tommy does, cuz he's not here to do it, so I'm doin' it for him," she declared showing a very determined expression while she waited for her mother to get the treat.

Amy sighed heavily choking back a sob, rose and went to the cupboard and retrieved the apple butter and brought it to the table. "Do you want me to put it on for you?" she asked.

"No, I can do it," Tammy said and reached for a spoon to apply the goodness.

. . .

WITH BREAKFAST OVER AND THE TABLE CLEARED, TOM fetched the family bible from the top of the sideboard and brought it back to the table. Amy and Tammy watched him as he flipped the pages to the Christmas story in Luke chapter two. He started reading, "And it came to pass..." and by the time he neared the end, Tammy was getting restless and when Tom read, " ...and the grace of God was upon Him," she jumped to her feet and went to the tree.

She searched all through the presents stacked under the tree but could not find any with names on them. Amy had purposely left off the name tags just to keep nosy eyes from doing any closer examination. Tammy turned with hands on her hips and said, "So, who gets what?"

"Well, young lady, you just sit right down there by the chair and we'll let your daddy hand out the proper presents," instructed Amy, stifling a giggle at the cuteness of her daughter.

"Humm, let's see," began Tom as he looked at the bounty. He lifted up one package, recognized it and handed it to Tammy. The parents watched as the excited little girl tore into the wrapping, trying to keep from tearing the simple brown paper and the red ribbon with a bow. Once she had it open, she saw material and knew it was the dress she asked her mother to make. With a broad smile, she looked at her mother and said, "Oh, thank you, Mommy."

Amy had knitted Tom a new scarf and socks, and the last present under the tree went to Tammy. When she opened it up, she hugged it to her chest and smiled at her mom and dad, "Oh, she's beautiful, Raggedy Ann!"

"Well, look further, there's something else in there," directed Amy.

When Tammy brought out the Raggedy Ann book, she held it up like a trophy. Amy had made the doll after the illustration in the book, red yarn hair and triangle nose and all. But when Tammy realized the doll had a dress just like her new one, she was so excited she jumped up and went to hug both her mom and dad.

When Tammy looked around, she said, "But mommy, you didn't get anything!"

"Oh, that's alright sweetheart, I don't need anything but your sweet smile."

Tom stood silently and said, "Uh, wait a minute," and slipped on his coat and hat and went outside. When he returned, she saw some fresh snowflakes on his shoulders but saw he was carrying a beautiful rocking chair he had been secretly crafting for the last two months and it sported a colorful ribbon bow at the top. She immediately forgot about the snowflakes and stepped to admire the handiwork of her loving husband.

Amy stood and put her hands to her mouth as tears filled her eyes, "Oh, Tom, it's beautiful! Set it down, I want to try it out!"

While Amy tested the rocker, Tom stepped back outside and came back in, holding the front of his coat as he turned to slip it off. When he turned around, he held a grey and black bundle of fur with two blue eyes and a pink tongue. Both Amy and Tammy stood with mouths gaping and Tammy ran to her daddy and said, "It's a puppy!"

Every step was a struggle for the short legs of the young boy, and without the help of Mama Grizz, he would have sunk into the snow and not made it more than a few yards. But he valiantly took one step after another, practically pulling himself free of the snow with his firm grip on the fur of the grizzly. After several minutes, the weakened Tommy had to stop and rest. He fell back in the snow and let the warm sun seep through his coat and warm his face. He hadn't eaten anything since the last of his berries and that was day before yesterday and water wasn't very filling and a mouthful of snow just gave him the chills. His chest rose and fell, and he closed his eyes to the bright sun. He was surprised to feel snowflakes on his face and he opened his eyes to look at the black bottomed clouds and then to his friend. Mama Grizz just sat back on her haunches and waited.

A few moments later, he pushed himself erect, looked to his furry friend, and said, "O.K. Mama, let's go some more." She dropped to all fours and moved beside the boy and the two started off again. A little way further and Tommy spotted what appeared to be a broken trail in the snow. This was the first sign of anyone he had seen, and his hopes soared. When they came near, he saw what he thought were tracks of a horse and the trail was headed out of the ravine to the lower ground beyond. The bear and the boy took the path of the already broken trail and Tommy found it easier going, relieved at their better progress. But he was still weak, and the exertion soon got the better of him and he had to sit down once again. He looked at Mama Grizz and said, "I sure wish I could climb up on your back and let you carry me, but... nah, better not." He sat on an exposed rock, and the lazy snowflakes drifted to his shoulders as he put his elbows on his knees and rested his chin in his hands. He felt the weight of the bag of rocks at his waist and thought about leaving them behind but pictured his momma's face when she saw the pretty stones and decided it was worth the extra effort.

When he felt rested, he stepped off the rock and joined his patient guide bear and started off again. As they walked, Tommy looked at the tracks in the snow that were slightly obscured with the dusting of fresh snow, and thought there was something familiar about them, then he realized these were not horse tracks, but the narrower tracks of a mule. "I bet that was Pa lookin' for me! Yessir, I bet it was! And he didn't know he was breakin' trail for us, Mama Grizz, but I sure am glad he did, aren't you?" The big bear turned her head around to see what all the noise was about but never missed a step.

———

"Oh, Papa, he's so pretty!" declared Tammy as she reached to pet the puppy, who licked her hand. Tom held the puppy closer and the little furball licked Tammy's face.

Amy looked at Tom, smiling, knowing they had talked about a puppy, but didn't know he had found one for them.

He saw her questioning look and explained, "He's one of the Hutchinson's pups. Joe brought him by the other day and I've been keeping him in the barn. He like's Bossy's fresh milk."

Amy reached over and stroked the pup's head, smiling, and asked Tammy, "So, what shall we name our new puppy?"

"How bout... uh, Tommy Too?" she asked innocently.

"No, we can't sweetheart, this puppy is a girl puppy," explained her Dad.

"Oh, I dunno, what do you think, Mommy?"

"Well, let's see, she's got blue eyes so how 'bout Blue?"

"That's a color, not a name," answered the little blonde.

There was a little silence as everyone thought about a name and Tammy tried to take the puppy from her father's arms, but Tom knelt down and set her on the floor, so the girl could get closer. She looked at the puppy and back at her mom and said, "I know! We'll call her Patches, cuz she looks like she has patches all over!"

Her parents looked at one another and Tammy giggled as Amy said, "I like it!"

"So do I!" declared Tom. Everyone stretched out on the floor and began playing with the inquisitive pup, laughing at his antics and anxious licks, enjoying the time together.

———

THE SUN HAD BARELY CRESTED THE TOP OF THE mountain off Tommy's right shoulder and struggled to show through the falling snow when they came to the mouth of the wide gulch. Tommy stopped and looked at the valley below. In the distance, he could make out the tree lined little river, the wide pasture and the few houses beyond. He searched for something familiar and finally saw the top of the barn that stood near his home. He smiled and looked at Mama Grizz, pointed to the barn and said, "That's home, Mama Grizz, that's home! We're gonna make it!"

He nudged her forward and they started off the long slope of the alluvial fan at the mouth of the draw. They had already come well over a mile from the cavern, but the distance remaining, although not through deep snow, was farther still. Once out of the trees and into the edge of the valley, Tommy's legs gave out on him and he fell to the ground. He was breathing heavily and gasping for air. He had forced himself to take each step and now the weakness from not eating was taking its toll. He rolled to his back and looked up as Mama Grizz dropped her nose to his face, as if asking what was wrong with the boy. He reached up and rubbed behind the ears on the big head that was almost as big as his whole body, but he felt no fear from his friend. "Just gotta rest a little, Mama, just let me rest a little." She sat back on her haunches to patiently wait for this little cub of hers.

As he felt the snow getting heavier, he knew he had to force himself to move, and he rolled over to grab at the fur of Mama Grizz and said, "You're gonna hafta pull me up, Mama." She gently rolled to her side and leveraged the boy to his feet, pausing to let him get his strength mustered, then started her slow ambling gait, practically dragging the boy with her. Tommy started counting to himself, "One, two, one, two," making himself lift his feet and move forward. Each step was as hard as the next, but he counted a cadence, pictured himself as his Pa in uniform and marching off to war, and took another step and another.

Tommy wasn't very conscious of where they were going, he just trusted Mama Grizz to lead the way. The bear, of course, was not one to go through gates and chose her route around the bottom of the pasture where the gravel from the gulch fanned out and the floodwaters had carved their way to Little River. With every step she took, she dragged the boy who held fiercely to the fur now with both hands and he stumbled along beside the beast. The snow was beginning to color her white and Tommy's eyes were clinched tight to keep the flakes from his eyes. His feet were beginning to numb with the cold and he buried his face in Mama's fur, but still he moved.

Suddenly, the bear stopped, unmoving, and Tommy lifted his face to see where they were. He was surprised to see they were in the trees just beyond their barn. These were the cottonwoods and ponderosa that served as a windbreak and now they caught the new fallen snow and stood white and silent. Tommy looked at the bear, let loose of her fur and took a couple of steps toward the barn, stopped and turned around to see the grizzly still unmoving, watching. The boy walked back to his friend and reached around her neck and hugged the wooly beast, speaking softly in her ear, "I love you Mama Grizz, thanks for bringing me home." Tears were chasing each other down his cheeks as he stepped back and looked at his friend. He dropped his head and turned away and started toward the house. He had gone no more than a few yards, when he turned back to see Mama Grizz standing up to her full height, pawing the air with her big padded paws and claws, looking as if she was waving goodbye to Tommy. He smiled through his tears, and waved goodbye to his friend. She dropped to all fours and ambled back into the trees and disappeared into the white blanket of winter.

When he got to the porch, it was all he could do to drop to his hands and knees to make it up to the door. When he got to the door, he struggled to stand, using the door jamb to help and the door handle. He leaned against the door frame and with his bare hand, he slapped against the door and tried to call out, but it was only a soft, "Pa, Ma, open..."

"What was that?!" asked Amy as she looked at Tom. "Did you hear that? There's something at the door!" She drew her knees underneath her as she started to get up.

Tom had rolled to his side and was getting up and looking at the door, "I didn't hear anything. But, I'll look," he answered and started to the door. He reached for the handle and slowly pulled the door open to see the frail figure before him, and immediately threw the door wide open as he hollered over his shoulder, "IT'S TOMMY!!!"

Amy ran to the door and both Tom and Amy caught the boy as he fell toward them. They hugged him close, unmindful of the door and Tammy ran to their side, wanting to hug her brother too. Both parents were bawling and rocking back and forth on their knees as they held their son, blubbering and trying to talk but the only thing that could be understood was, "Thank you God, thank you, thank you!"

Finally, when they slowed their jubilation, Tom kicked the door closed and looked at Amy, holding the boy tightly and letting the tears flow freely down her face, smiling, laughing, crying, letting every emotion be released as she kissed her son all over his face. Tom patted the boy on his legs and shoulders, running his hand up and down his back and saying, "It is so good to see you boy, so good." He stood and looked down at his caterwauling family and laughed with the long pent-up emotions and danced a jig of joy around the three.

Tommy had said nothing, just let his tears flow and hugged his Ma and held his sister's hand. Then he feebly said, "I'm hungry."

Amy pulled back at looked at her son and said, "Your sister made us save some pancakes for you, would you like some?" He nodded his head and tried to get up, stumbled and staggered but grabbed the back of the chair and pulled himself into it to wait for some food.

The rest of the family were seated around the table and watched as he slowly took bite after bite, stopped to breathe a little and sip on some cold milk, then eat a little more. When he had finished a stack of three pancakes he asked, "Could I have some more?" Amy looked at Tom and he said, "Better wait a bit, if you eat too much too fast, you'll just bring it back up."

"I'm tired," he muttered and pushed his plate aside, dropped his head to his arm on the table and was fast asleep.

Tom and Amy looked at the boy and at each other as Tammy asked, "Shouldn't he be in bed?" Tom stood and picked up the boy, carried him into their bed and Amy folded back the quilt and Tom lay the boy down. He didn't stir but slept through it all and Tom and Amy stood in the doorway, smiling and watching him sleep. Finally, they stepped back and quietly closed the door and walked back to the table, with smiles that split their faces and holding hands with one another. Tammy was back on the floor playing with the temporarily forgotten puppy and the parents happily watched, finally at peace with everything.

As they watched Tammy playing with Patches, Amy went to the stove and picked up the coffee pot to refill their cups. Once his cup was full, Tom raised it to his lips and started to blow on the hot steaming brew but made a face instead. He sat down the cup, brought his hand to his nose and sniffed, scowling and jerking his head back. He looked at Amy and asked, "Do your hands smell?"

She frowned at him, smelled her hands, then her dress and said, "It must have been Tommy. Wherever he was, it must have stunk something awful, that is disgusting. I'm going to heat up some water now and wash up, you need to wash as well, especially if we're going to church!" With the big pot of water on the stove, she tiptoed into their bedroom to fetch some fresh clothes for the two of them. Once inside, she leaned over the prone form of Tommy and easily verified he was the source of the odor. When she came out with the clothes, she said, "We're going to have to wash that boy, head to foot, he's rank!"

Tom looked at his wife with a sober expression, "Uh, there's something you need to know. Something I kept from you, so you wouldn't worry." He dropped his eyes before continuing as Amy lay the clothes on the table and sat down opposite her somber faced husband. "I think what you're smelling is Grizzly."

Amy's eyes flared wide and color drained from her face, "What do you mean, Grizzly?" she demanded.

"Well, that first day when we found Tommy's .22, there were grizzly tracks right close by and it appeared the Grizz might have dragged the boy away."

"You knew that, and you didn't tell me?" she asked as she leaned toward him, fire in her eyes.

"Well, I didn't want to worry you. What good would it have done for you to know that?"

Amy exhaled slowly, staring lightning bolts at her husband, and gradually relaxed to sit back in her chair. She dropped her head and softly replied, "None, I guess. It's probably just as well I didn't know and you're right, I would have worried myself to death." She lifted her eyes to Tom and said, "You know me too well, even better than I know myself, sometimes. So, that's why he smells?"

"Probably. Bears have a particularly strong odor anyway, but a hibernating bear, well, with all the urine and such, they get pretty rank," explained Tom.

Amy's hands were in her lap and she stared at them, as she breathed in she caught another whiff of the smell and wrinkled her nose. She looked to Tammy and said, "Tammy, could you take the puppy into your room and close the door, we're going to change our clothes and Tommy's sleeping in our room, so it'll just take a few minutes."

"Alright, Mommy. C'mon Patches, let's go to my room." She picked up the pup and carried the furball into her room and shut the door.

Tom suggested they wait till after they gave Tommy his

bath for them to wash up and change clothes, knowing they would have to handle both boy and stinky clothes to get him scrubbed and changed. Tom brought in the bathtub and they began to fill it for the boy and once they were ready, Tom went to the bedroom and brought out the still sleeping boy. They quickly undressed him and sat him in the tub, the warm water comforting to the boy and he lay his head back and snoozed while they washed him all over. It was only when his Mom started washing his hair that he started paying attention to what was happening. "Whoaa, the warm water felt good, that's the first time in a long time I've really been warm, but you're gettin' soap in my eyes!"

When they finished with the boy, he asked, "Can I have some more pancakes?"

Both Tom and Amy laughed, and she went to the stove to fix him another stack of flapjacks. While she was busy with Tommy, Tom went to the bedroom to wash and change. When he came out, clean clothes and smelling a lot better, Amy went in to freshen up herself. They had agreed not to question the boy on his experience but would wait until he was ready to share the tale in his own way. Tom was certain when the truth came out, the story would be a doozy.

It was an excited and happy family that climbed aboard the wagon that Christmas morning to go to church. Tammy and Tommy snuggled down under the quilt in the back of the wagon and Tom and Amy seemed to sit closer than ever before, taking warmth from one another. They were a little late, understandably so, and Tom just hitched the horses to the corral fence and the family walked up the church steps together, dusting the snow off as they entered the church.

The pastor's wife, Rebekah, was at the piano and the

congregation was singing Joy to the World when Tom opened the door for them to enter. The usual curious folks turned to see who was so late getting to church and big eyes over gaping mouths showed surprise. Elbows and whispers passed through the crowd like a tidal wave and the broad smile of the pastor as he led the singing was all that preceded the tears that started down his cheeks. He dropped his hands and the music stopped and everyone turned to see Tommy walk slowly beside his father as they went to the open seats a couple rows from the front of the church. Mumbles and praises could be heard, and handkerchiefs flashed as cheeks were dried until Grandma Chappell, everybody's favorite old saint, lifted her hands and shouted, "Praise the Lord!" and "Amens" and "Hallelujahs" filled the church building.

The smiling pastor, with a handkerchief in hand and tears still flowing, stood before the crowd and lifted his hands and said, "Folks, we have a Christmas miracle! And I think the song we were singing is the most appropriate for the moment. Join together as we sing, Joy to the World." Rebekah had rushed to Amy's side and gave the joyful mother a warm hug and then asked her to take the piano, which Amy gladly did.

Once the singing was over and everyone seemed to be settled back in their places, the pastor took the pulpit and began, "My text this morning is from Matthew, chapter 2, and verse 12. Actually, just the last two words, *another way*. This is the passage that tells about the wise men having come to see the Christ child and giving their gifts, but after seeing Jesus, they went home another way. You see my friends, throughout Scripture we find that God guides us. Sometimes in ways and places we wouldn't choose ourselves, but He's always there with us and guiding us, just like he guided Tommy home to his family. And when someone truly comes to Jesus, there is such a change in their life that they go home *another way*. II Corinthians 5:17 says that when we come to Christ we become a *new creature* and that *old things are passed away; behold all things are become new*. So, my question for you today is, when you came to Jesus, were you changed? Or did you hold on to old things like habits and secret sins? Let Jesus make things new in your life this Christmas, give your life to Him and He will give you the gift of eternal life."

When the pastor dismissed the services in prayer, the chatter throughout the crowd was focused on their Christmas miracle. The pastor was the first to ask Tom, "What happened?"

Tom shrugged his shoulders and with uplifted eyebrows and open hands, he said, "I dunno, pastor. We decided to let Tommy tell us in his own time and the only thing he's said so far is 'I'm hungry' and 'I'm tired'."

"Well, how did you find him?" asked J.B. as he pushed to the front of the crowd that surrounded the family. Tommy was sitting beside Amy in the seat and was asleep on her shoulder, but it was evident by his dark sunken eyes, and the deep sleep, the boy had quite an experience.

Tom replied, "He found us. We heard something at the door, and when we opened it, he fell into our arms. That's all we know so far." He looked back at his sleeping boy and turned around to the pastor and the others, "We're just very thankful for all of your prayers and your help, we couldn't have made it through without all of you, our church family."

The crowd soon dispersed, still talking about the big event of the day and the pastor walked the family to their wagon. Tom carried Tommy and set him in the back of the wagon beside Tammy who covered him with the shared quilt. He turned to the pastor, "I'll let everyone know the details as soon as we learn them if we ever do. And again, pastor, thank you and everyone for your many prayers, there's no doubt that this is an answer to prayer." He climbed up into the seat and backed the wagon away from the corral and turned to the road, waving to the remaining families, and started back home. The snow had let up and the sky was clearing, promising to be a beautiful day. With only three to four inches of fresh snow, it was a white Christmas, but not a bad storm.

Tommy slept all the way home and when they were inside, he turned to the ladder to the loft, looked back at his Pa and Tom said, "How 'bout you just using Tammy's bed for now. Go ahead in there and get some rest. We'll wake you after a bit and you can have some Christmas dinner, how's that?" He forced a weak smile and pushed the door open to his sister's bedroom and disappeared.

Tom had bagged a couple of prairie chickens and Amy had already stuffed them with a cornbread stuffing and they were roasting in the big cast iron dutch oven in the stove's oven. The delightful smells filled the house and Amy sat in her rocker as Tom teased the puppy with his stockinged foot. "Do you think he'll ever tell us?" asked Amy, thinking about Tommy.

"Oh, I'm sure the story will come out sooner than later, but he's had quite an experience and we need to just let him tell it as he will. Who knows, once he gets rested up and stuffed with your good cooking, he'll probably run off at the mouth and talk about it so much we'll get tired of listening."

"I don't care, I'm just so glad to have him back home. I

was beginning to give up hope, and I know if you had told me about the grizzly, I would have given up a long time ago!" She shook her head at the thought, "But, from what you said, and the way he smelled, he must have been pretty close by the bear, don't you think?"

"Probably, but don't go worryin' your head about it, there's nothing to be done now."

"You're probably right," she answered and got up to check on her dinner. She turned back to Tom, "Could you get that heavy pot outta there for me, please?"

"Sure babe, glad to help," answered Tom and stooped to bring out the big pot with the two potholders provided by his wife. He sat it on the top burner plates and Amy used the lid lifter to check on the roast chicken. She turned with a smile and said, "It's ready, and by the time you get the young'uns to the table, the rolls will be ready too."

Everyone enjoyed the meal and talked about Christmas, church, and everything but Tommy's adventure. The only words Tommy spoke were, "May I have some more?" Both Amy and Tom were a little amazed at the boy's appetite, but both were pleased he was enjoying the meal. When he was finished, he leaned back in his chair and looked around the table at his family and smiled. A quick frown wrinkled his forehead when he asked, "Where's my bag?"

"Your bag? What bag?" asked Tom.

"The one I carried my biscuits in, you know, the drawstring bag."

"Probably over there in the pile of your clothes with your coat an' all," answered his Pa, pointing to the pile of clothes near the door.

Tommy jumped up and went to the pile, digging through it until he found his bag. When he grabbed it, he hefted it and smiled. He turned and walked to his Ma and said, "That's your Christmas present." He handed it to her and when she took it, she almost dropped it.

"That's heavy! What is it?"

"Open it. They're for your flower garden," he declared, anxiously waiting for her to see the surprise.

She pulled at the opening, loosening the drawstrings and looked in, then reached in to find her gift. She withdrew one of the fist sized stones and held it in her palm and looked back at Tommy, "Oh Tommy, it's beautiful! These will look wonderful in my garden. Where did you find them, I thought there was snow everywhere?"

"In the cave," he said, matter-of-factly, as if was nothing of concern. "There's more, but I got the prettiest ones."

"Oh, they are pretty. This is quartz, isn't it Tom?" she asked as she set one on the table in front of her husband.

He glanced down and said, "Yeah, looks like it. It's a nice white..." he paused and reached out to pick up the stone. He turned it over and over and looked at it very closely. He picked at it with his finger, rubbed it clean and looked a little closer. "Let me see another one of those," he said, with a bit of a frown wrinkling his forehead. When Amy handed another one to him, he examined it as closely as the other one and lifted his eyebrows and looked at Amy. "How many of those are in that bag?"

She reached in and retrieved all the stones and lined them out before her. There were six stones, all about the same size and had little variation in color. Some of the quartz had a slight touch of pink to it, but most was white with the streaks of what Tommy thought was Iron Pyrite.

Tom let a smile stretch his mouth and his dimple poked a hole in his cheek as he asked Tommy, "Do you know what that is?"

Tommy looked at the stone again, now in the better

light coming through the windows, and picked one up and said, "Well, I first thought it was mica like you told me about, but when I could see it better, and that different color, I figured it was that iron pyrite you talked about, you know, fool's gold."

"Well, you're right in your thinking, and it's a pretty good guess. But if you look closer, fool's gold had sharp edges and shapes, but that doesn't. And the color, when you wipe it like on that first stone there, is brighter than pyrite. What you have there is genuine gold!"

Amy and Tommy both looked at the stones and each picked up one of them to examine it more closely. Amy looked at Tom, "Are you sure? It's gold?"

"I'm sure. And what you have there, oh, I'd guess, might be as much as eight, maybe ten ounces. That's mighty rich ore." He looked at his son and asked, "Do you think you could find that cave again?"

Tommy sat down and thought, then looked up at his Pa, "I dunno. I wasn't awake when we went there, and when we left, I wasn't looking back, so I dunno."

Amy and Tom looked at one another, both having caught Tommy's use of "we" when he spoke about the cave. But both looked back at the stones and at one another and smiled when Tom said, "Even that is enough to go a long way toward paying the bank. We have a bigger miracle than even we thought." He looked to Tommy again and asked, "Uh, son, when you said you weren't awake when *we* went there and when *we* left. Who did you mean when you said, we?"

He dropped his head and said softly, "Mama Grizz, she saved me and helped me."

Amy let the tears fall and pulled Tommy close to hug

him tight. She looked at her husband as tears filled his eyes and said, "Is that what you call a Christmas Bear?" Tom smiled and nodded his head as he pulled his big red hanky from his pants pocket and wiped his eyes and blew his nose like an out of tune trumpet, making everyone laugh.

IT WAS SEVERAL DAYS AFTER CHRISTMAS BEFORE TOMMY began telling his family about his time in the mountains. He spoke timidly, quietly, trying to remember all that happened, but he thought there really wasn't much to tell. It seemed so natural that he had become friends with the bear, not unlike the way Tammy and Patches bonded. He said she slept most of the time and the first time he tried to leave, she stopped him, but he knew later that if he had gone out into the storm and cold he probably wouldn't have survived. He smiled when he spoke of sharing his biscuits, "I think she liked 'em even better'n me! I just wish I'da had more." He looked at his Pa and said, "An' I saw where you'n Meg had come up a ways and broke trail for us, too!" They knew he had to be keeping something back, but they could only wait for him to tell them in his own time, but as the days passed, there was nothing else to share.

When school started again after the holidays, Tom asked Tommy's teacher, Mrs. Parks, to try to keep the others from asking too many questions and she agreed to do the best she could. However, when the others accused Tommy of lying about the bear, he began to withdraw and spent more time by himself. It was during that time that Amy thought her son passed from being a little boy to a young man, no longer dependent on the approval and presence of others. But he was still her diligent and loving son at home and a good brother to his little sister. Tammy, after all, believed everything Tommy said and saw her brother as a brave and courageous man of the woods. Tommy smiled and laughed at his sister's hero worship but was always attentive and protective of her.

When the trees started to bud, and the weather turned warm, the pasture grass showed green and his Ma's flowers started pushing through the dirt, Tommy asked if they could go for a ride as a family. Tom looked at Amy and she nodded her head and said, "Let's! I'll fix up a picnic lunch and we'll just go to the mountains and pick some flowers and enjoy the scenery!"

Tom and Tommy went to the barn to ready the horses while Tammy helped her mother pack the picnic basket. They were soon on their way and when they cleared the pasture, Tommy pointed Meg up the draw that was familiar. Tammy and Tommy rode double on Meg and Tom and Amy were aboard the pair of horses, with the picnic basket tied on behind the pommel of Tom's saddle. They let Tommy lead the way and he found the game trail that cut across the face of the east facing slope above the bottom of the draw. There was a little water still flowing in the bottom from the high-up snow melt, but the warm sun of the spring day was a welcome relief after the long winter. Tommy pointed out some of the spring blossoms of golden pea or mountain sweet pea, some little white star lilies, and some tall fuzzy pasque flowers. When they neared the end of the draw, the trail angled up the hillside and they saw some of the aspen starting to bud out.

He found a shoulder of the hillside that was well covered with bunch grass that was starting to green up and would be appreciated by the animals, and the sun brightened a wide smooth area for their picnic. While Tommy and his dad picketed the horses, Amy and Tammy spread the blanket and readied the meal. They had a great view of the valley below where their ranch lay and the distant valley and mountains beyond. It was a relaxing time and the family was enjoying the getaway.

Tommy took his chicken leg and walked to the edge of the shoulder to look down into the narrow draw below, uncertain if that's where the cave that had been his refuge was hidden. He had thought long and hard about whether to even try to find it again, wondering if he would see Mama Grizz or not and if she would remember him. He wanted to see her, but he didn't want anyone else to find her. He was afraid what would happen to her and what she might do around others. He had pretty well resolved himself to keep their cavern a secret and just treasure the memory.

He tossed the chicken bone down the hill, knowing there would be plenty of scavengers, both furry and feathered, that would enjoy the treat. He turned to walk back to his family who had sat watching him quietly, and something moved that caught his eye. He shaded his eyes and looked to the top of the ridge and smiled. He spoke to his family and said, "Hey everybody! Come look!" They jumped up and came to his side and looked in the direction where he pointed. There, at the top of the ridge, just over a hundred yards away, a big grizzly bear followed by two little fuzzy cubs, had just crested the ridge and stopped and turned. The big bear seemed to be looking down at them and didn't move for the longest time as the cubs caught up with her. She stood up to full height, and most would say she had smelled the men and horses and was getting a better look, even threatening, but once again, Tommy was certain she was waving at him as she pawed the air with her forepaws and Tommy waved back and whispered, "Bye, Mama Grizz." She dropped to all fours, turned to look at her cubs, and the fur family disappeared over the ridge.

Tommy and his family stayed looking, saying nothing, and then each looked at Tommy who seemed to have grown at least a foot in their eyes, and smiled as they hugged him and one another. All the way home, not a word was spoken as each one treasured in their hearts what they had been blessed with, and each in his own way, determined they would never forget the Christmas Bear, and Tammy hugged her brother just a little tighter as they rode home together.

*A LOOK AT: TO KEEP A PROMISE
(BUCKSKIN CHRONICLES BOOK 1)*

The power of a promise made and a promise kept is realized when Jeremiah Thompsett comes of age and accepts the responsibility of fulfilling his mentor's long-held dream. Raised by an escaped slave in the midst of the Arapaho nation in the Wind River mountains, he now must track down the slave catchers that killed his adopted father and stole their cache. The Vengeance Quest takes him and his companions through the mountains and across the nation to fulfill the promise of freeing the family of slaves held dear to his mentor and adopted father.

Accompanied by Broken Shield and Laughing Waters, his Arapaho friend and his sister, the trek through the mountains and to Fort Union is fraught with hazard and ambush. It is here he is joined by Scratch, the crusty mountain man who joins him on his journey downriver and across country to find Ezekiel's family and to seek to free them.

AVAILABLE NOW ON AMAZON

Born and raised in Colorado into a family of ranchers and cowboys, B.N. is the youngest of seven sons. Juggling bull riding, skiing, and high school, graduation was a launching pad for a hitch in the Army Paratroopers. After the army, he finished his college education in Springfield, MO, and together with his wife and growing family, entered the ministry as a Baptist preacher.

Together, B.N. and Dawn raised four girls that are now married and have made them proud grandparents. With many years as a successful pastor and educator, he retired from the ministry and followed in the footsteps of his entrepreneurial father and started a successful insurance agency, which is now in the hands of his trusted nephew. He has also been a successful audiobook narrator and has recorded many books for several award-winning authors. Now finally realizing his life-long dream, B.N. has turned his efforts to writing a variety of books, from children's picture books and young adult adventure books, to the historical fiction and western genres which are his first love.

Find B.N. Rundell at:
wolfpackpublishing.com/b-n-rundell/

Stay up to date on future releases, specials discount offers and more. B.N. Rundell's Mailing List:
https://bnrundell.com